That's No Place for a Girl!

A Novel

Graham Duncanson

Copyright © 2023 Graham Duncanson

All rights reserved, including the right to reproduce this book, or portions thereof in any form. No part of this text may be reproduced, transmitted, downloaded, decompiled, reverse engineered, or stored, in any form or introduced into any information storage and retrieval system, in any form or by any means, whether electronic or mechanical without the express written permission of the author.

This is a work of fiction. Names and characters are the product of the author's imagination and any resemblance to actual persons, living or dead, is entirely coincidental.

Cover design by Scott Gaunt Graphic Design: scottgaunt@hotmail.co.uk

ISBN: 9798392793860

Also, by this author

Francesca
Anna
Katie
Emily
Polly
Three Lovely Girls
Lucy
Freda
Jenny
Sarah
Fighting for Liberty
Ruth
Liberty Comes at a Price
The Sinners
Catherine's Crazy War
Una Walks with The Elephants
Una's Second War
Saving Lydia
Sylvie
Afsoon
Emma
Annabel's Vow
Annabel Tries to Be Normal but Fails
Frostie Talks in the Shower

THE MATING LIONS' TRILOGY
Mating Lions
Fiona
The Scream

Abbreviations

ACP	Acetyl Promazine
ADVS	Assistant Director of Veterinary Services
AHITI	Animal Health and Industrial Training Institute
CAIS	Central Artificial Insemination Centre
CBPP	Contagious Bovine Pleural Pneumonia
CV	Curriculum Vitae
DC	District Commissioner
DDVS	Deputy Director of Veterinary Services
DLO	District Livestock Officer
DO	District Officer
DVO	District Veterinary Officer
DVS	Director of Veterinary Services
EAA	East African Airways
EATRO	East African Trypanosome Research Organisation
EAVRO	East African Virus Research Organisation
ECF	East Coast Fever
FMD	Foot and Mouth Disease
GBH	Grievous Bodily Harm
GK	Government of Kenya
HMS	Her Majesties Steamship
HQ	Head Quarters

LMD	Livestock Marketing Division
LO	Livestock Officer
LPO	Local Purchase Order
ODA	Overseas Development Agency
PA	Personal Assistant
PC	Provincial Commissioner
PPL	Private Pilot's License
PVO	Provincial Veterinary Officer
UK	United Kingdom
UN/FAO	United Nations/Food and Agriculture Organisation
VIO	Veterinary Investigation Officer
VO	Veterinary Officer
WW2	World War 2

Characters in order of appearance

In England

Tanya. A newly qualified veterinary practitioner in mixed practice

Louise. A veterinary nurse

Mr. Grimshaw. A partner in a mixed veterinary practice

Mr. Griffiths. A partner in a mixed veterinary practice

Mr. Halliday. A partner in a mixed veterinary practice

Mr. Jones. A dairy farmer

Nat. His cowman

Archie. His teenage son

Mrs. Jones. His wife

Mrs. Cavendish. An elderly horse client

Malcolm. Lister. A pig farmer

Gwen. His wife

Jackie. A smallholder

Jane. A veterinary nurse

Mr. Jackson. A calf rearer

Mrs. Peabody. A dog client

Rick Gimmer. A thief (alias Mr. Gaston)

Unnamed accomplice

Unnamed Police Sergeant

Len. A police constable

Phillip. A cowman

Charles Cunningham. A wealthy estate owner, who owns a beef herd and breeds horses.

Jill. His wife

Sally His eldest daughter

In Kenya

Stanley. A UN/FAO driver

Morton. His son employed as a turney boy.

Terry Stokes. Director of Veterinary Services (DVS)

Michael Levin. Deputy Director of Veterinary Services (DDVS)

Judy. His wife, sister to Helen White

John Adams. Assistant Director of Veterinary Services (ADVS) Field

Charles Shaw. Assistant Director of Veterinary Services (ADVS) Laboratory

Kipchoge. His cook.

Matua. Tanya's cook

Niels Lindstrom. UN/FAO Project Leader

Elisabeth. His wife

Trudi and Gretel. His daughters

Joseph. His driver

Zebedee. His son employed as a turney boy.

Dick White Head of the Livestock Marketing Division (LMD)

Helen. His wife, sister to Judy Levin

Zak. His driver

Marco. His cook.

Horatio Little. Chief Zoologist.

Anthony Banks. Chief Librarian

Percy Gibbon. Farmer and microlight owner

Rune. Head of Centre of the Artificial Insemination Service (CAIS)

Margit. His wife

Astrid and Britta. His daughters

Susan. Hockey player

Martha. Hockey player

Eve. Hockey player

Ricki. Rugby player

Jeff. Rugby players

Karissa. Mombasa Veterinary Department Driver

Silas P.A to The Provincial Veterinary Officer Coast Province

James Roberton. (PVO) Coast and North-eastern Province

Jacob Messenger in Mombasa Veterinary Office

Chris Patten. Mare at Miritini near Mombasa

Angela and Alan Barret. Hockey hosts who live at Nyali

Sealion. Boat Driver at Mombasa ski club

Tim Stockman. PVO Eastern Province

Mohamidi Basu. PA to PVO Eastern Province

Hadi Basu. His brother Tim Stockman's cook

Captain James Fairbrother. Machakos rancher

Barnabas Toya. Kabete Farm Manager

Benjamin. The head boatman in Lamu District

Saul. The assistant boatman in Lamu District

Mr. Suleiman. DLO Lamu District

Peter and Darki. The Proprietors of Petley's Hotel

Kasim. Senior Veterinary Scout Lamu District

Mabrouk. Driver Lamu District

Abdi. Clerk/microscopist in the Lamu Veterinary Office

Ali. Messenger/microscopist in the Lamu Veterinary Office

Justin. LO Sabaki

Ngonjo. James Roberton's cook.

Joan and Rachel. Wives of Machakos rugby players

Axmeed. DLO Wajir District

Mathew Clarkson. Shipping agent with Smith Mackenzie

Reg Pertwee. Nanyuki Farmer

Daniel Toya. Chief Veterinary Scout at Garsen

Kiptoung. Samburu Headman

Brian. A flying instructor

Chapter 1

I woke up on a cold winter's morning in early 1962 and I was not quite sure where I was. I was naked, lying on my tummy. At least I was alone, heaven forbid that a guy had seduced me last night. Surely, I had not had that much to drink. The telephone beside my bed was ringing. I reached for it, as I realised that I was in a flat which was above the branch surgery where I had just started to work as a qualified vet. I had had too many drinks last night with the two good-fun, vet nurses, Louise, and Jane. I had slept in.

It was Louise. She had obviously guessed that I had slept in. She giggled, "I expect you are just coming down! Mr. Grimshaw has been on the phone. He would like you to pick up the calving at Mr. Jones of Broadhaven Farm."

There are three partners in the mix practice who employ me. Mr. Griffiths and Mr. Halliday are both old school large animal vets. They think all large animal vets should be like them and be male, have barrel-like chests and stand over 6 ft 2 inches. Basically, they do not rate me and if they had their way would never send me out on a large animal call. They also think that they have a right to look down the front of my shirt to check that I haven't got a barrel-like chest. This infuriates me. To both excite and to spite them, I normally keep the top button of my shirt done up and don't wear a bra.

Mr. Grimshaw is basically a small animal vet, but thinks he is an expert in large animal medicine and surgery. He does his utmost to avoid going out on any farm calls particularly those first thing in the morning. He will have taken this call at 7.00 am as he is on duty, but he will have sat on it until I come on duty at 8.30 am.

I am in a complete panic. I thought that I would have been doing morning surgery. It is going to be freezing outside. It is cold enough in my bedroom. My bottom is frozen just sitting on the lavatory. I can't seem to find any knickers, but I do find an old vest which I used to wear when I was fifteen. It is much too tight now, but I don't want to spoil any decent clothes. I always get filthy trying to get calves out of cows. On goes an old track suit and three sweaters. I am a great believer in layers. At least I had the sense to bring my overalls and wellies in last night, so they are not sub-zero. Captain Scott who I secretly admire as he was a bit of a loser like me, would now be proud of me, as I bravely go outside, putting on a ridiculous Peruvian hat which a friend had given me after her gap year in South America. It has flaps that cover my ears. I know I look like a pixie.

I am under five foot. I have always been intimidated by big men. My father who is a farmer and my two brothers who are both older than me, are brown-haired, blue-eyed giants. My mother has similar genetics. I on the other hand am a real blond and have dark brown almost black eyes. I suspect my mother had a fling with a visiting brush salesman. It can't have been the milkman as we kept cows and we did not have a need for one. We just dipped a jug in the bulk tank!

I scrape a square of ice off the windscreen. At least there was no snow in the night and the Vauxhall Viva starts. I set off into the gloomy morning which is made worse by my poor ice scraping. I do not enjoy going to Mr. Jones, he and is cowman, called Nat, are both big. I am told that I have a cheeky attractive smile. It is very difficult to smile at anyone when you are terrified of them and of the situation that you are in.

I park beside the milking parlour. As I get out, I hear Nat's teenage son, called Archie, shout, "They have sent the girl! I need to leave for school. Bye."

Thanks to the Peruvian ear flaps I mercifully don't hear the exact expletive from within, but I suspect it was describing a part of my anatomy. My heart sinks further as I remember that I have left my waterproofs in the washroom at the practice. I will have to manage in my overalls.

I suppose enormous men with arms as long as a gorilla's might be better at drawing calves out of cows than me. However, I am manually dextrous, with small hands and arms. I have considerable strength in my fingers and forearms. I think overall I am more useful. I am ace at getting lambs out of ewes. Men particularly big men never give me any credit. They write me off before I have even tried. I have learnt that the best thing is to tell them exactly what I am planning to do and how they can help using their marvellous strength which in my experience is normally inadequate.

I arrive at the door of the calving box. Nat is inside trying to catch the cow. I try to smile but I know it probably looks like a grimace. Mr. Jones says, "We have been waiting for you for nearly two hours. I rang when we finished milking at 7.00 am."

I had been dead right with what I thought had happened. I answer with as much loyalty as I can muster, "I am sorry, Mr Grimshaw got tied up with another case. I didn't come on duty until 8.30 am."

There is a crash from inside the calving box as Nat fails to catch the cow. If they had been waiting for two hours, why ever didn't the catch the cow?

I enter the calving box and try to smile at Nat saying, "Let me help you, Nat, in fact could you get me a bucket of hot water. I will have a go at catching her." He does not even reply but stomps out.

I like cows and they in their turn tend to trust me. I suppose it is because I talk quietly to them and move slowly. Perhaps I am a pixie. I soon have got the chain around her neck. I don't make the mistake of using the hook on the chain, as, if she goes down suddenly, you are likely to be unable to release it and she will throttle herself to death. I tie the chain with some bailer twine in a quick release bow.

I turn to see Mr Jones watching me, "Not just a pretty face, are you?" Suddenly the darkness has been lifted out of my life. I can smile. He smiles back. I ask, "What has she been doing?"

He answers, "I saw her straining when we had finished milking. She has had three normal calves before, so I reckon, she has a problem."

That's encouraging at least there has not been an enormous arm insider bringing in bacteria and causing inflammation. Nat returns with the bucket of hot water. I pour in some disinfectant, get Mr. Jones to hold her tail and I clean her vulva. Then having pushed up my sleeve and washed my arm, I push my right arm into the cow's vagina.

I turn to Mr. Jones, "You were right, there is a problem. The calf is coming backwards in a full breach presentation. I will need to get right inside her to straighten out her back legs. Then it is vital that we draw the calf quickly before it drowns."

Mr. Jones says, "You had better get the calving aid Nat and the short ropes."

I felt myself once again being drawn into a dark place. It is cold in this calving box, and I need to shed some clothes. I am going to be freezing. I get out of the top half of my overalls and tie the sleeves around my waist. Then I must take off my numerous layers. I drape them over the hay rack on the wall of the box. When I have got down to my vest. I look up. Both Mr. Jones and Nat seem mesmerised. Surely, they have seen a girl striping down before. Obviously in this part of Wiltshire it must be a rarity. On reflection, my vest without sleeves is rather skimpy and perhaps not wearing a bra is rather provocative. I have no time for further reflection, it is time to bring my experience and training into practice.

I tell them what I am doing, "Because my arms are slim, I'm going to put them both into her birth canal. Then I can push back on one of the calf's hocks with one hand and grasp the foot of the other leg with my other hand cupping the foot to keep it flexed."

I now have got my whole body up against the cow and because I am working, I am not nearly so cold. My face is pressed up against the cow's anus. I look up straight into the eyes of Mr. Jones who is holding the cow's tail so that it is not in my way. Our eyes meet. We both smile. I manage to draw the leg into extension and out of the cow. It is much easier to draw the second leg out as I have slightly more room inside the cow.

I am firmly in command now. As I put the two short ropes on to the calf's back legs above the fetlocks, I stress, "It is vital that we get the calf quickly out as soon as we put tension on the ropes with the calving jack. As you are stronger than me Nat can you work the handle. I will hold the pole."

I get the first smile out of Nat which I have ever seen. Everything happens very fast. Nat is working the jack as fast as he can. I am holding the calf to my body to stop it falling to the ground violently. At last, the calf's head comes out of the cow's vulva, the cow collapses on top of me. Mr. Jones releases his hold on the cow's tail, as there is no way that he can hold her up. He reaches out to the bailer twine and releases her neck. She is fine and can lie on her side and breathe normally. On the other hand, I am on my back. My body and legs are trapped under the cow.

Mr. Jones grabs me under my armpits and drags my clear, leaving, my tracksuit bottoms, my overalls, and my wellingtons under the cow. I scrabble to my feet dressed in my tight vest and my socks. We all laugh, and I ask, "I hope you won't get into trouble from the council, Mr. Jones. I doubt if you have a license to run a nudist park! Let's make sure the calf is breathing OK." To my delight the calf shakes its head.

Mr. Jones replies, "I have got to hand it to you Tanya you are not only a good vet, but also a bloody good sport. Nat help me get the poor girl some clothes before she catches her death from cold."

When these are retrieved and I have got my wellington's back on, I clean up my arm and feel inside the cow, saying, "I will just see if there is a twin?" Sure, enough there is one. However, this one is coming headfirst in the normal manner. I have no trouble drawing it out of the cow without the need of any ropes or the calving aid. Then the three of us sit the cow up on to her brisket and pull the calves around to her head so that she can lick them.

I see Nat looking at them and ask, "What sex are they?"

He answers, "Both heifers."

Mr. Jones says, "That's lucky. It is so sad when one is a bull and the other is a freemartin heifer, and therefore infertile."

I reflect, "I think that it only happens in cattle. Twin lambs are normally fine. It is extremely rare for sheep to have freemartins. I think that I will give the cow a long-acting injection of penicillin as I did have to put my arm insider her. However, you will be withholding the colostrum from the bulk tank anyway, so you won't have to throw any milk away."

Mr. Jones puts his hand on my shoulder in a nice way. I find it interesting that I can always tell if a man is touching me up, "You think of everything Tanya. Thank you for your help this morning. Nat and I are going in for something to eat. Would you like to join us? I couldn't help but notice that you forgot to put on any underwear. I guess you were in a bit of a rush and did not get time for any breakfast."

I reply, "You are right. Yes, I would love some."

This was a real first. I had never been invited in for a meal before. Mrs. Jones is a lovely lady, and I am given a plate of porridge before a full English breakfast which included black pudding. I was pleased that my nudity earlier was not mentioned. I reflected how I had managed to brazen it out in the cowshed with two men, but I would have been acutely embarrassed if the topic had been mentioned in front of Mrs. Jones. What happens in the cowshed, stays in the cowshed!

By the time I returned to my home at the branch surgery, Jane had arrived. The heating had been turned on and the warmth has percolated up to my flat. I have a lovely hot bath and hair wash. I have time to dry it before my first appointment so for once I look very presentable to the small animal clients. My day continued on a high until I arrive at the main practice. Mr. Grimshaw had got behind with his appointments like he always does, so I am drafted in to help him to catch up.

This is a complete nightmare as all the clients want and expect to be seen by him. They either think that I am schoolgirl or a complete imbecile. There are some advantages. The clients who want to see Mr. Grimshaw tend to be either fussy older clients or ladies who have got nothing else in their lives other than their rather snappy miniature poodle. The clients who agree to see me are wanting a quick fix; young mums with young children who need their dog vaccinated, wealthy guys with lame shooting dogs or older men who have been sent in by their wives with the cat no one in the household is interested in, or finally the really sad cases where the old pet has come to the end of its life and needs my help to reach its creator, with as little pain and discomfort as possible. At least as these cases have not been allocated a time, I can take some time to be kind to both the owner and their animal. These cases take away all the good feelings that I have taken on board by being appreciated by Mr. Jones and send me into a spiral of despair.

I wonder why I am doing this job. I love being a vet but not one who is inside. I realise that I don't mind being freezing cold, with no clothes on, in a cow shed. That is exciting and gives me an adrenaline rush. Seeing pets belonging to owners who don't want to see me is the complete opposite. It is depressing. I am therefore delighted when Jane sends me out to remove the tusks from a boar.

This time I remember my waterproofs which are dry, and I put on my boots which are spotless having been brushed in hot disinfectant in Mr. Jones' dairy. I had done this operation before with an old practitioner when I was a student. He was my hero. He always let me do things and he was very encouraging. His mantra which became mine was, 'A strong woman is a lot better than a weak man'. I put the horse molar cutters, a long instrument which I had used before in my car. I knew that my best option was to creep up on the boar when he was asleep and do the job which was totally painless while he continued his slumbers. However, my back up plan which my mentor had taught me was to cut the boars tusks off while he was serving a sow. I remembered the twinkle in the boar's eye as he was thrusting away enjoying himself and I was relieving him of his aggressive weapons which he had been using to injure his sows, not to mention the fear he had given to the pigman. Apparently, every year somewhere in England, a pigman is killed when a boar charges between his legs and severs his femoral arteries.

I was just going out the door when I am waylaid by Mr. Grimshaw, "Will you be alright Tanya,"

I reply but I know that I'm not going to get away with my answer, "Yes, I will be fine."

"You know to use embryotomy wire?" My guide and mentor had told me two years ago that because tooth enamel is the hardest substance in the body, never to use embryotomy wire as it gets too hot and keeps breaking. I smile rather than argue with the fussy old woman. I once had been reprimanded by one of my favourite clients when I had apologised to her saying, "I'm sorry I'm late Mrs. Cavendish. I got held up by that old woman Mr. Grimshaw."

"Tanya, I am an old woman and I do not want to be compared with Mr. Grimshaw!"

Mr. Grimshaw still would not let me go, "You know the dosage for a general anaesthetic in a pig of that size?"

I nod my head indicating that I do know the dosage of anaesthetic for a big boar. This true, but I have absolutely no intention of giving the boar a general anaesthetic as they are terribly risky, often giving pigs heart failure, and are also very expensive. I do not want a telling off from Mr. Griffiths who always checks my invoices and complains if there is anything which seems expensive. This annoys me, not only because I resent being checked up on, but also because I know there is a massive percentage mark up on the cost of medicines which goes straight into the practice profits. Being a farmer's daughter, I do not like to see farmers being shafted.

At last, I get on the road for the three-mile journey to a hundred sow pig farm owned by Malcom Lister. I know he is struggling financially as he has recently purchased the farm from the council. He only has sixty acres of arable land which is not really a viable size. The pigs are a vital income stream. He works like a Trojan. Did Trojans work very hard? I seem to remember that they spent most of their time drinking and fornicating. Malcolm does neither of these, but he is always smiling. I like him.

Sadly, the boar is very much awake, so it is plan B. I can see with one look at him that he knows very well that there is a sow on heat in the pen next door to him. He is frothing at the mouth. I have a vision of Mr. Jones and Nat frothing at the mouth as I stood naked in front of them earlier this morning! Luckily the vision quickly fades. I wave the three-foot-long molar cutters as Malcolm grinning like a Cheshire cat opens the door separating the two pigs. I am rather cross with the boar. The sow is standing rock still with a resigned look on her face and yet, he whacks her bottom with his head inflicting a wicked six-inch cut which mercifully is not that deep.

With a grunt he mounts her, thrusting his corkscrew penis through her vulva. I don't delay. I have four tusks to cut. I quickly cut the two near to me. Then I must get around the other side of the copulating pair. There is not much room between them and the wall of the sty. I am naturally rather nervous having my backside towards the boar. I remember the cut in the sow's bottom. I'm brave and get on with the job.

I am very relieved to get out of the sty and leave them to their lovemaking. As I am washing my boots in a bucket of disinfectant, Malcolm hands me one of the boar's tusks which he has picked up off the floor. It is five inches long and the edge is as sharp as a razor. I thank him and say, "I think I will get a friend who makes jewellery to set it in a silver mount and wear it around my neck as a pendant." This makes him a laugh. I don't think he realises that I am serious.

We go in to have some tea and cake with his wife Gwen. The practice has rung through another call to her to hand on to me. It is only five miles away. A pet sheep which is off food. It did not sound too urgent so I felt I could allow myself quarter of an hour to enjoy the cake and Gwen's company. She like Malcolm was often smiling. I think she is relaxed because now her two children are at school.

I made use of their loo before I left to go to see Jackie at Walnut Cottage. Wearing overalls makes having a wee a real mission.

The sheep in question is called Rupert. He had been castrated as a day-old lamb before being bought by Jackie and reared on the bottle. He is very friendly and behaves rather like a dog. He is allowed into the kitchen. He is now six months old.

He looks very sorry for himself. Jackie who is a good-looking woman in her mid-thirties is very concerned. I know she and her two sons aged six and eight are devoted to Rupert. I take his rectal temperature thinking that he probably has a fever. He doesn't but I feel a diagnostic sign. Just below his anus I could feel his urethra. It was throbbing. I did not need any lecture from Mr. Grimshaw. I knew Rupert had a blocked urethra somewhere between where I could feel the throbbing and the end of his penis.

I had to treat Jackie like a farmer. I was rather relieved that her sons, who were always asking questions were away at school. I started my sex education lecture which I found awkward enough giving to Jackie. I would have been as red as a beetroot if I had been giving it to the boys as well, "Sheep like all ruminants do not get an erection by a swelling of the penis. They have a S-shaped penis so when the ram wants to inseminate a ewe, small muscles contract so that the penis doubles in length. He thrusts it into the vulva and the insemination is all over in seconds."

Jackie laughs, "I feel a bit sorry for the ewe not having any foreplay."

Suddenly I feel rather hot in the kitchen which is heated by a large Aga. I wish I hadn't got so many clothes on. Why I don't stick to the matter in hand, I'm not sure, but I tell her about the foreplay of the boar which resulted in a cut in the sow's gluteal region. I feel even hotter when Jackie says, "I like a lot of foreplay and enjoy Robert, smacking my bottom and nibbling me with his teeth. I am glad he does not have tusks like a boar. It would be so embarrassing taking him to the doctor to get his tusks removed. You are so brave Tanya dealing with great big boars."

I feel on safer ground when I get the conversation back to sheep by saying, "Poor Rupert has got a blockage in his penis, and he can't spend a penny. Now we need to somehow relieve the blockage. I will just get some instruments from the car."

I was pleased that I sounded so confident, but actually I was very nervous. My real concern was Rupert's welfare. I knew the approach which Mr. Grimshaw would take, as I had seen him do it. He would inject some local anaesthetic under the skin below the anus and into the musculature of the urethra. Then having surgically cleaned the area he would make an incision and expose the urethra. This would enable him to make an orifice for the urethra under the rectum and allow Rupert to urinate like a female sheep. In theory this was a useful bit of surgery and solves the problem. Sadly, in reality it normally does not work very well, and the patient tends to get urine down its legs. Its fleece gets sodden and smelly. This, in the summer, attracts blow flies which lay eggs. These hatch into maggots which eat into the flesh. The whole thing is then a very painful disaster. I don't want Rupert to suffer in this way. In my opinion it would be better to put him to sleep now to spare him the pain. I am not sure if Jackie will see it in the same way as me.

I had read about a clever idea being done in India using a catheter with a blow-up cuff around its end which you can insert through the sheep's flank. You leave this in place while you dissolve the stones in the blockage. Then in a few days you remove the catheter, and the sheep is back to normal. I knew I would not get any support from Mr. Grimshaw doing this, particularly if it all went wrong and I would have to admit that I had never done the procedure before.

I came back into the kitchen with a sterile set of instruments. I hoped that I would be able to alleviate Rupert's problem with something simpler. I sit Rupert on to his bottom and then get Jackie to hold him sitting up like a dog. Then bending down beside Rupert, using both hands I have to get him to be a bit excited which makes Jackie giggle. I hold the shaft of his penis very firmly with one hand in the area just in front of his scrotum. Obviously, he has not got any testicles as he was castrated months ago. I have to push his penis forward so that the tip comes out of his prepuce. Then what joy, I can see a small stone lodged in his vermiform appendage on the tip of his penis. Dextrously I cut off the blocked appendage with a pair of sharp scissors. Jackie then has urine spotted with blood spraying all over her kitchen floor. Rupert to my pleasure has a very relieved look on his face as the puddle of urine gets bigger. Jackie is not quite so pleased with the mess, but when I tell her that I have saved Rupert from having a very expensive and painful operation she is pleased.

I explain that Ruppert does not need his vermiform appendage but from now on she must but some ammonium chloride in this food, so his urine is more acidic. She asks, "Why have sheep got vermiform appendages?"

She seems to find it amusing when I reply, "No one really knows for sure. The accepted wisdom is that when a ram ejaculates it wriggles about and helps to spread the semen around the ewe's cervix. I hope it just tickles the ewe to give her a little pleasure!"

Chapter 2

All in all, a very successful call. I am back on a high again as I return to the main surgery. Surprise, surprise, Mr Grimshaw is running late again. Actually, I am relieved as he won't now have time to lecture me about my calls this morning. With Jane's help, I set about castrating three cats, spaying three further cats and castrating an apparently over sexed terrier which spends its whole time trying to hump the client's husband's leg.

Jane and I are a well organised team so we can gossip while we work. Jane tells me the reason for Mr. Grimshaw getting behind, "He has been playing with his box of dog bones. He is worse that an African witch doctor!"

I ask, "Has he got an orthopaedic op this afternoon?"

She laughs a little hysterically, "It is a cruciate op on an old pug. He always gets himself into a state before a cruciate operation. I am worried stiff about the anaesthesia. I hate intubating flat nosed dogs."

I try to encourage her, "I will give you a hand. We can only do our best. I wish the profession could stop them being bred."

Louise comes in, "Thank goodness old Grimblebones has left for his lunch. Well done getting all the routine surgery done."

I look at the clock. It is 12.45 pm. Hopefully old Grimblebones won't be late back from his lunch. He normally is. At least us girls can relax as we certainly won't see Mr. Griffiths or Mr. Halliday before 2.00 pm. We all knuckle down and get the operations room and the two consulting rooms clean and tidy. I do all my booking, Jane and Louise get ready for the cruciate operation.

We eventually get a fifteen-minute sit down to have a cup of tea and eat some biscuits.

Mr. Grimshaw arrives back at 2.15 pm and goes into the partner's room, Through the open door I can see him playing with the dog bones. I must be fair to Mr. Grimshaw, he is a very good surgeon. In fact, if I am honest, he is better than most of the surgeons at Veterinary College and he is not slow. His problem and it is my and the nurse's problem is that he will not get started. Eventually at 2.30 pm I can stand it no longer and go into the partner's room, "Mr. Grimshaw would you like me to anaesthetise the pug? I could even do the op if you want me to?"

He replies, "No, no Tanya, it is much too tricky for you. I see there are four calf castrations at Mr. Jackson's why don't you do them?"

I am delighted, "Great, I will ring him and get going."

I feel sorry for Louise and Jane as they are still hanging about when I go out of the door. Louise gives me a look to say, 'Bloody man'.

Mr. Jackson is not my favourite client but at least I am out of the surgery. It's still cold but the sun is shining. I get the call done in an hour. I get the thumbs up from Louise as I pass-by the open operating room door. The pug is on the operating table and Mr. Grimshaw is scrubbing up. The two other partners are in the partner's room, so I quietly go into a consulting room and read my latest Veterinary Record after doing my booking. I look rather longingly at the job adverts. Soon I am consulting again in an open surgery with Mr. Griffiths. We each call a client in. I am aware that Mr. Griffiths tends to duck out into the partners room whenever he can. At the end of the surgery when the door is locked at 6.30 pm, I have a client with me, and I hear Mr. Griffiths leaving. When my client has left, I walk into his room and see that he has only seen five clients in the two hours. I have seen twelve. I know I am only an assistant, but the inequality in the amount of work annoys me. I also know that I am bringing in well over my share of the turnover.

Mr. Griffiths then adds insult to injury. He is first on call and has gone home to have his supper. He rings through to the surgery as Louise has put the telephones through to his home and asks to speak to me, "Are you still at the surgery?"

Through clenched teeth I say, "Yes, I have just seen the last case."

He asks, "I hope you don't mind. I have just told Mrs. Peabody that she can bring her dog in for its annual vaccination as she is off early on holiday tomorrow and needs him vaccinated to drop him off at the kennels."

I am speechless and then manage to say, "Yes I do mind." Then I realise that he has put the phone down. I will have to wait for her to arrive. I wearily go to the door and unlock it so that she can come straight in. It is another twenty-five minutes before she arrives. I have calmed down by then. She is a nice woman and has made a genuine mistake. I greet her warmly thinking, 'Bloody Mr. Griffiths. He should have come back to see her.'

Then I must smile as she gives me a box of chocolates. She knows that I have gone out of my way to help her. I thank her and say how Jane, Louise and I will have a chocolate tonight now that we have finished for the night. I know one person who is not going to get a chocolate. I suggest to Louise that she hides them away from Mr. Griffiths.

Sadly, that is not my last case for the evening. I go home to my flat above the branch surgery, make myself an omelette, have a shower and go to bed. I am a lucky person. Sleep comes easily to me, and I am soon in a land of dreams.

I am rudely awaked by a phone call. It is Mrs. Griffiths, "Reg said he thought that you could pick up this call as he will probably have to go out to Mr. Meekins, to a calving. A Mr. Gaston is coming in with a sick cat to the main surgery." There is a click as she puts down the receiver. It is only when I am putting on my clothes that I realise that I have been used once again. Mrs. Griffiths only said that a calving was a possibility.

Mr. Griffiths could easily have seen the cat first. Now I will have to go back to the main surgery and open up again. It would have been much more convenient for me to have seen the cat at the branch surgery under my flat. I would not have had to go out into the cold. I am so cross I stamp my foot. This was a mistake as I was just putting on my knickers, I lose my balance and fall over. Luckily my sense of humour surfaces and I smile and finish dressing.

I arrive at the main surgery. There is no sign of Mr. Gaston. I turn on all the lights and open the front door. I am keen to sort out the cat and get back home to go to bed again. A pick-up truck draws up and two men get out clutching a bundle in a black polythene bag. This does not look promising. The men are big and overweight, and my grandmother would describe them as, 'very unsavoury my dear'. I would go further than my grandmother. They look terrifying. I open the door. As I am ushering them in, I say, "What's happened to your poor cat?"

Mr. Gaston says, "It was hit by a bloody hit and run."

When I have a look at the cat in the bag, I see that the poor old thing is very dead. By the smell he has been dead for several days. I am seriously angry but manage to be very professional, "I am sorry to tell you that your cat has died, Mr. Gaston."

Because I had been looking at the cat, I had not noticed that the other man had moved behind me. It was a big mistake. He grabs me from behind with one arm around my neck and the other round my waist, ripping off my skirt. "I am glad to have a wrestle with you my pretty one."

Now I am terrified. I remember being told on our first day at veterinary college that if you are molested that it is important to scream and make as much noise as possible. I'm silent as I can't see the point. I know I am totally alone and know no one will hear me.

Mr. Gaston unlike his partner has his mind on other things. He demands, "Where are the takings?"

His question allows me more time to focus on a plan. I answer, "In the till."

"Where is the bloody till?"

"If you let go of me, I will show you?"

I am well aware that there is only a float of £5 in the till, but the whole days takings and in fact the last three days takings are in the dangerous drug cupboard.

Mr Gaston, I was sure that was a false name, nods his head and his accomplice releases me. My initial terror and indeed anger has reduced, and I am now using my brain to get myself out of this mess. I walk through to the pharmacy which contains the till.

The pharmacy is a narrow room with shelves on either side over two long work tops. On the work top opposite to the till, Mr. Halliday has left his twitch. I hate this particular instrument. A normal twitch is a two-foot-long broomstick with a loop of thin rope on one end. It is a device to control a horse. The rope noose is tightened around the fleshy nose of the horse. This releases natural endorphins into the bloodstream of the animal and gives up to quarter of an hour of calm in its demeanour. Mr. Halliday's twitch is very cruel. It has a heavy ring of stainless steel around one end of a very heavy pole, through this runs a chain which is tightened around the horse's nose causing excessive trauma.

At that moment of time my thoughts were on self-preservation and not on horse welfare. Mr. Gaston was not looking at me. He was looking at the till. His accomplice was behind him and could not see me. I grabbed the twitch and hit Mr. Gaston on his head with all my strength. I think technically I had poleaxed him. He crumpled. This gave me time to swing the twitch at the surprised man behind him. He went down but was not totally out for the count. I hit him again. This time with more precision. I could see he had lost consciousness.

I jumped over the two bodies and ran into the practice office. I got a real buss of excitement as I dialled 999. Immediately the call was answered, "Which service do you require?"

I answered, "The police."

A voice replied, "I am putting you through."

There was a click, a slight pause and a firm male voice said, "Wiltshire Police. Please give me your name and address."

I replied, "This is Tanya Fox at The Veterinary Surgery on the Bath Road in Chippenham. My telephone number is Chippenham 8430."

The voice asked, "How can we help you, Miss Fox?"

I answered, "I have been attacked and assaulted by two men who were trying to steal the takings."

The voice replied, "I will send two cars round immediately. I suggest you vacate the building and run away if you are in any further danger."

I was impressed by the police, by the time I had left the building I could hear the siren. I walked to the gate of the surgery car park which was, as normal, wide open. I could see the blue light. I walked out into the road and stood shivering. I realised that now I was in a state of shock. I took several deep breaths to calm myself. It was only then that I realised that I had lost my skirt and was only in my knickers. Then I smiled. I knew my mother would be pleased as I had put on a clean pair!

I stood aside as two police cars came swinging into the car park. Four police officers jumped out. One who I guessed was a sergeant shouted, "You two go round the back. Len, you come with me through the front." I seemed to be superfluous, so I just followed Len.

The two men were lying where they had fallen. There was a large puddle of blood. I certainly had hit them hard, but I had no regrets. I was relieved that they both seemed to be breathing. There was a thumping on the back door. I asked, "Shall I let your men in Sergeant?"

He replied, "Thanks luv."

Len said, "Sarge, isn't that Rick Grimmer who we nicked a couple of years ago for GBH?"

I was hurrying to the back door, so I did not hear the sergeant's reply. I was worried the two police officers were going to bash the door down. I shouted, "Hold on I'm coming."

The banging stopped and the two police officers burst in as I unlocked the door. While they gawped at the bodies in the pharmacy, I retrieved my skirt and put it on. I tied a long calving rope around my waist to keep it up.

The police officers are none too gentle with Mr. Gaston and his accomplish who wakes up while they are dragging him out of the front door. The Sergeant turns to me, "You did well Miss. Can you come down to the station in the morning to make a statement?"

I reply, "I have two calls first thing in the morning. Will it be OK after that?"

He nods, "I will have finished my shift by then but one of my colleagues will help you."

I thought, 'That is typical. They work eight-hour shifts. I have been on duty and yet I have to go to work in the morning as normal.'

The police then leave. I must clean up the bloody floor. I think, 'Typical men leaving a woman to clear up after them.'

In the morning I go straight to my first call which is a dairy routine at Manor Farm. I like the cowman, Phillip. He has a cheeky smile. I catch him reading the Sun newspaper. He is ogling the girl on page three.

I greet him with, "You should have been at Hill Farm yesterday. I gave Mr Jones and Nat a full frontal as I was calving a cow with a breech delivery."

Phillip laughs, "Next time you come, I will get you to do the same here. It will save me buying a paper."

I answer, "Dream on Phillip."

I find it amusing that I can flirt with guys like Phillip and know that he will never do anything untoward and yet Mr. Gaston and his mate are really dangerous. I am cross that I did not realise that immediately, that I saw them. I should never have opened the door without checking on them from an upstairs window.

The cows are quiet well-behaved Ayrshires. They are chained up in a long cowshed. Phillip has a wooden box for me to stand on which makes it much easier for me to do rectal examinations on account of my short stature. I am sure the cows like me examining them rather than a great big man with massive arms. I am checking certain cows which have not been seen to be on 'bull' for more than 8 weeks after being served. If they are in-calf I will not actually be able to feel the calf as it is smaller than a mouse, but I will be able to feel the slight swelling in one of the horns of the cow's uterus. It is an exact procedure and needs care. I am proud that I am very good at it. Phillip records on a pad which cows are pregnant. If they are not pregnant, I am supposed to tickle their ovaries to make them come on bull. I am sure this is rubbish, but as it does not hurt the cows, I am happy to tickle them. I also feel inside cows which have had their calves more than six weeks ago but have not come on 'bull'. I check that their uterus has contracted down to a normal size and does not contain any pus which is usually creamy and smelly. If I find a cow like this, I wash it out with a dilute solution of iodine. The other vets give the cow an injection of a synthetic female hormone called stilboestrol. This makes the cow appear to come on 'bull' which pleases the farmer. I have noticed that any cow which has received this injection continues to come on 'bull' but is never fertile. I never give this injection because I am sure that it is bad for the cow. Instead, because I must give her something to please the farmer and my employers I give her an injection of vitamins. This injection does not do any harm. However, I do suspect that it doesn't do any good. I am now doing a little research. I keep my own records of the injections and washouts which all the vets give to these infertile cows. I hope it will lead to some improvements in how we treat them in future.

While I am doing these examinations, I am wearing a parturition gown. This is waterproof and does up at the back. It comes up my neck to my chin. It has short sleeves which are tight around my biceps. In theory this should stop dung getting on to my clothes. It is rarely successful. The washing machine in my flat is constantly working. As my arms get covered in dung or pus, they are always smelly and often dark green or brown. At the end of a session, I stand with my arms out and Phillip delights in hosing me down with the pressure washer. I am certain that in his mind I am in the nude like the girls in the 'Sun'.

My second call is a similar routine. It is not so enjoyable as the cowman is very dour. He is kind to his cows so I do not dislike him, but I do wish we could have a laugh and a joke occasionally.

I clean up as best I can before I go to the police station. I know I must smell of cow dung but there is not much I can do about it. A sergeant behind a desk helps me to make my statement. It is lucky that I am not shy as he gets me to record some quite intimate details. I am not looking forward to appearing in court. He tells me that the two men have been kept in the cells overnight and will come up before the magistrates later in the morning. They will then be remanded in custody until they are tried in a month's time. I am beginning to dread that.

The statement has taken quite a time so that it is noon before I get to the main surgery. Mr. Griffiths is not pleased by my absence, but I can't see why, as he is back at the surgery after is morning round so, he can't have been too busy. I explain about last night and about having to go to the police station, thinking that this information would mollify him. It doesn't and I get sent out immediately to castrate a yearling colt which he could easily have done because Louise has boiled up the instruments in anticipation of him doing the call. I am sure it is meant as a punishment. In fact, it isn't as it is job which I enjoy doing and which I think that I am good at. I have done twenty-two colt castrations. I have recorded them all and I hope to use the information to give a short paper at the annual equine congress.

The practice policy which I think is a good one is to do them all under a short acting anaesthetic. Louise has prepared everything that I will need in a wooden box. I put it in my car and set off. I have never met the owner before. He is a big farmer who has arable land and a large herd of Hereford suckler cows. I have been to the cows but have only seen the cowman, predictably called Hamish, as he is a highlander with a very broad Scottish accent. I have never met the governor. He breeds heavy hunters. I have been instructed to meet him at the stables. I drive up to a very imposing house and have a fit of nerves, as I drive around the back of the house to the beautiful old stable block. I wish I didn't smell of cows.

The client is a large imposing man and my heart sinks even further. To my surprise he comes and opens my car door and says, "You must be Tanya. I was expecting to see Mr. Griffiths, but I'm pleased that you have come. I have had a very good report from Hamish of the wonderful things which you have done for our cows." I am so delighted with this greeting that I feel like kissing him. He holds out his hand and I give it what I hope is a firm shake. I blurt out, "I'm sorry I stink of cows."

Mr Cunningham says, "You must not worry about that. It shows that you are a working girl. I think I am a man ahead of my time as I believe in the equality of the sexes." He laughs, "How could I think differently with a very formidable wife and six wayward daughters."

I like him even more now. I notice he has got a severe limp as we walk to the stables. I see a steaming bucket with a towel ready beside the stable containing my patient, a big quiet bay. Mr. Cunningham unhooks the leather head collar beside the stable and we both enter. The horse stands rock still as Mr. Cunningham puts on the head collar. I take my stethoscope out of my pocket, saying, "He is a good looking fellow. I will just have a listen to his heart and have a feel to make sure he has got two testicles and nothing else in his scrotum." The horse continues to stand still as I examine him.

Mr. Cunningham then leads the colt out of the stable across the concrete, through a gate into a small grass paddock. I come along behind and bring the bucket and the towel. I then return to my car to collect the castration box with everything which I require. I put the box down and shut the gate. The last thing I need is for my patient to pull away from his owner and gallop off on to the farm.

I say, "I am just going to give him a pre-med of Acetyl Promazine, often called ACP."

Mr. Cunningham laughs, "I think we gave the troops ACP tablets when they boarded the landing craft on 'D Day', to stop them feeling sick."

With astonishment I say, "How amazing that you were at 'D Day'. I am mad keen on history. I have read so much about it."

He replies, "I don't remember much after the ramp went down. I was leading my men up the sand and was hit in the leg. At least I can say that I was there. My family say that I should try to forget as we want peace in Europe now."

I said very positively, "I don't think we should forget the horror brought about by the Nazis. We need to remember so that we never let such a dreadful thing happen again."

He murmurs, "My thinking entirely."

Now I replace the leather head collar with my soft-cotton, halter. I have heard a story of a head-collar buckle damaging the facial nerve. I start getting all the injections ready. I gauge that the colt weighs 700 lbs. He is well grown.

Now the ACP is beginning to take effect. I very quietly, using a small-bore needle, inject some local under the skin where I have clipped away some hair over the jugular vein. Now he won't feel the large bore needle which I need to insert into the vein. Blood starts dripping out of the needle. Now I need to be quick. I inject the anaesthetic Thiopentone first, followed by the muscle relaxant, Succinylcholine and finally a small injection of Nikethamide which will stimulate the horse to breathe. I take out the needle. I hope I won't need to give any more anaesthetic. I know I must be quick. I grab the towel and put it around my neck like a prize-fighter.

I come round in front of the horse pushing Mr. Cunningham out of the way, saying, "I will take him now." I hold both sides of the halter to try and prevent the horse rearing and going over backwards. Mr. Cunningham steps back laughing, "I can see you know exactly what you are doing young lady. I will await further orders."

I thank my lucky stars as the colt collapses down quietly and I roll him on to his side, putting the towel half under his head to protect his lower eye and then bring the rest of the towel over his upper eye so if he does wake up, he is in the dark. Then I say, "Can you kneel on his neck, Mr Cunningham. I don't want him to get up until we have finished. I know he has had some of his tetanus inoculations, but I will give him a booster just to make sure."

I hear him say, "Very wise."

Then I run back to get my bucket. I pour in some hibitane and drop a bottle of acriflavine into the bucket so that it is warmed and will flow easier. From the box I take a short length of rope attached to a single hobble. I slip this over the pastern of the upper hind leg keeping out of range of a kick. I give it to Mr. Cunningham, knowing he is safe on the dorsal side of the neck, asking, "Can you pull his leg forward?" I wash my hands in the bucket and put in a small clean towel, which I then use to wash the area of the scrotum.

I bring the stainless-steel fish-kettle containing the boiled sterile instruments out of the castration box and place it by the tail of the horse so that I can reach it from behind the rump. I take the scalpel in my left hand and squeeze the lower testicle hard into the scrotum. I make a long incision over the testicle through the skin and all the tunics. The testicle pops out. I put the scalpel in the fish-kettle and grab the emasculator saying quietly to myself, "Nut to nut." The emasculator is an instrument which clamps on one side and on to other side near to the nut it cuts. The testicle is attached by the tunics at one end. I severe them with the emasculator. Then I severe the vascular end and hold the emasculator in place for a full minute counting the seconds under my breath. I repeat the procedure with the second testicle. I pour acriflavine into both incisions.

I amuse Mr. Cunningham when I pick up the two testicles and throw them into the hedge. I ask him to relax on the rope so that I can remove the hobble. I place all the gear and the bucket near to the gate. I then reach out my hand to help him to get up.

He says, "Thank you my dear."

We walk together to the gate. I laugh, "I always stand with the owner outside of the field so that they are not tempted to run to the horse when he makes attempts to get up. There is no way a man, however strong can hold up a 700 lbs horse." We lean on the gate and wait. I ask, "Can you tell me more about 'D Day'?"

"I was an experienced officer having fought with my men at Dunkirk and then in North Africa. 'D Day' was still very frightening particularly in the landing craft with the guns of the capital ships firing salvos over our heads. The only good thing was that we had total air supremacy and so unlike in the other theatres of war we were not constantly checking the sky for enemy planes. In fact, there was little German resistance in our sector when we hit the beach. I was just unlucky to be hit, or perhaps you could say lucky as I am still alive."

He was silent looking into the distance with glazed eyes. I said, "Thank you for fighting and saving us from a dreadful tyranny."

He turned to me, "I am grateful for that, Tanya. No one has ever thanked me for fighting before. You would have made an excellent officer. I noticed how you had everything so well planned and prepared this morning."

We said no more as the horse with a massive effort got to its feet and stood like a table with a leg at one corner. Then it took a couple of shaky steps before putting its head down to graze. Mr. Cunningham mused, "I wonder what that young chap is thinking."

I replied, "I don't know, but I never have had a horse bear me any malice after being castrated, so I don't think they remember anything."

Mr. Cunningham chuckled, "Just as well. We won't disturb him. I will collect the towel later and take off your halter. Would you like to join my wife and I for some lunch?"

"I would love to."

He had given me an insight into his wife's character which was very accurate. Their daughters were all at school, so it was a very orderly lunch. I could image with six girls that it normally would have been a riot. I made my departure rather hastily as I knew that I was in for a busy afternoon at the surgery. I did remember to pick up my halter. I reflected that when an operation went according to plan, veterinary surgery was very satisfying.

There was nothing satisfying in the afternoon. Mr. Grimshaw was running behind. I was fully booked and did my best to keep up with my appointments. As soon as I thought that I might get a break the receptionists would give me one of Mr. Grimshaw's appointments.

A week later I got a letter by special delivery summoning me to court. I had to attend at 11.00 am. I got the receptionists to write in the daybook that I was not to be given any appointments after 10.00 am and that I was to be given no outside calls. I had no intention of going into court looking a wreck and smelling of cows.

I was called into the partner's room. All three of them were present. Mr. Halliday took the lead, "Tanya, we are not at all pleased with your attitude. We have seen the note in the book for next Wednesday. It will put the partners under considerable pressure. You should have asked permission to take a day off."

Normally when I was being given a dressing down, I would stand up straight but keep my eyes down. Not today. I looked him straight in the eye and said, "I have no intention of taking a day off. I was assaulted on a call back to the surgery which I never should have been asked to do. I was second on call. Mr. Griffiths should have taken the call. He was first on call and was at home."

Mr. Griffiths went very red, "I was waiting to go to a calving cow at Mr. Meekins."

I was not having that, "A call that never materialised. I have looked on his account. You never left home."

Mr. Halliday asked, "Is that true, Reg."

He stuttered, "Yes she had her calf without any assistance." They stood there looking like three goldfish. I turned on my heal and left the room. It was then that I decided that I would start looking for another job.

My court appearance was not as frightening an experience as I thought it would be. Both barristers treated me politely and sympathetically. I was made to tell my full ordeal. The judge requested me to tell him about the twitch. When I explained what it was and that it just happened to be on the counter, he accepted that there had been no preparation on my part. The men were convicted and would be sentenced in a week's time. I read in the papers that they both got ten years. I had absolutely no sympathy for them.

All the junior staff who in fact were all female backed me to the hilt. I never had a day taken off my holiday entitlement. It did not stop me from looking in the Veterinary Record at the job section every week.

Chapter 3

Like all of us I do not relish change, but my mind was made up. I liked the area and so it was a pity that I knew that I would have to move away. I would miss the staff, many who were good friends. I would not miss my employers who I no longer trusted or respected. I also had spoken to two of my best friends from veterinary school. They both were getting bigger salaries and had more time off. I would miss most of the clients particularly the farmers and smallholders.

One of my concerns was that I perhaps was jumping out of the frying pan into the fire. How would I get a better job. I knew salary was not everything, but it did indicate appreciation. I was not brave enough having been qualified for less than two years to set up on my own. I did not have sufficient capital for a start. Also, it would mean that I would be on duty 24/7 for at least two years before the work built up enough for me to employ anyone else.

When I carefully analysed what I really wanted, I knew that I wanted to work outside with large animals. If I was honest, I really wanted adventure. That is why I read in detail about a job in Northern Kenya working with camels. It was a United Nations/Food and Agricultural Organisation (UN/FAO) funded project. There would be a Project Director based at The Government Veterinary Laboratories at Kabete which was near to Nairobi. The job which I was interested in was for a Kenya counterpart who would be a Kenyan civil servant. He would be paid the same as a normal government veterinary officer, but he would receive 25% extra salary paid tax free in the UK. The leave was amazing. He would only get 14 days local leave which was miserable, but he would receive 168 days overseas leave at full pay every two years. The reason for this was that the applicant would be working in a dangerous area. This sounded like a war zone. I would certainly get an adventure.

When I really thought about it, I knew that as a twenty-five-year-old girl I did not stand a hope in hell of getting the job. I did not think that there would be many applicants but as soon as they realised that I was a girl, my application would be put in the bin.

What I did not know was that The Overseas Development Agency (ODA) based in Stag Place in London who were the ultimate employer were having considerable difficulty finding a candidate. They were now under some considerable pressure from, not only The Kenyan Government, but also FAO.

My full name is Tanya Livingstone Fox. My mother was a Miss. Livingstone. I decided that I would lose the Tanya on my application form and just apply as Livingstone. T. Fox. This was never picked up at Stag Place. In fact, the recruitment officer decided that with a name like Livingstone I must be just the man for the job. Because there was some urgency for the recruitment, it was decided that I would have my rigorous FAO medical in Rome on my way to Kenya. I never went to Stag Place.

I flew from Heathrow on an early flight to Rome. I was picked up from the airport by a charming, Italian, FAO driver who insisted that I join him for breakfast. Then he parked in the underground garage for the FAO Building. This had been built by Mussolini to house his portentous office for administering his overseas colonies in the mid 1930's. The story goes that The UN bought it off the Italians after WW2 for one dollar as there was no other buyer.

My medical was extremely extensive. It included chest x-rays which I am sure were just so that they could see my breasts. No one thought to query that I was a girl. I passed with a clean bill of health and was taken back out to the airport by my charming driver who insisted that he took me out to dinner on the way. It was only later that I found out that he had collected a total refund on his expenses. However, I did not begrudge him the money as he had been very entertaining. Having passed my medical I had not needed any encouragement to imbibe quite a volume of fine Italian wine, so when I got on the East African Airways (EAA) plane which was almost empty, I had no hesitation in stretching out across three seats and covering myself with the standard airline blanket. I slept through the night time stop at Benghazi and only woke when we were made to put on our seat belts to land at Entebbe in Uganda. The sun was bright as I strolled around the airport. I was surprised that I did not have a headache from the wine. I took it as a good omen for the future. I sat on a bench in the sun and like a true tripper rolled up my shirt sleeves and hitched up my skirt to get as many of the sun's rays on my body as possible.

Soon we were ushered back on to the plane. Everything was delightfully low key. I started to enjoy the African way of life. I learnt some Swahili from my guidebook. I was convinced that I had done the right thing changing jobs. I imagined the bedlam at the surgery in Chippenham with Mr. Grimshaw running late as usual.

It was only an hour's flight to Nairobi. Embakasi airport was also in brilliant sunshine. As there were so few people on the plane, immigration was no problem. I found my suitcase and wheeled it on an airport trolley into the customs area. Then my troubles began. The two customs men were obvious slightly bored and insisted that I opened my over-full suitcase. They were not unkind but made me take everything out including all my underwear which seemed to amuse them. I guessed that their wives had rather fuller figures then mine. They really laughed when I had to sit on the case to get it shut again. At last, they were happy to put a chalk mark on my case. I only had to walk five yards to another man on the door who insisted that he got a glimpse of the chalk mark.

That was the last of the easy-going life I was expecting. Outside of the arrivals' door was chaos. Everyone and his cousin wanted to give me a lift into Nairobi. I was terrified that someone was going to steal my case. I held my handbag under my other arm as if my life depended on it. Eventually I saw a placard which made me smile. It was asking for Doctor Livingstone, sadly there was no PRESUME after the request. I managed to get near enough to the broadly smiling African to shout, "I'm Livingstone. Are you Stanley." He shouted back, "How did you know my name? I not expecting a pretty lady!" I smiled at him and pushed my way towards him. He grabbed my case and hefted it onto his shoulder. We then made satisfactory progress getting to the exit. Right outside guarded by two policemen was a big Landrover with red number plates which I later learnt meant a UN vehicle. Stanley opened the passenger door, winked at me, and said, "Welcome Madame Ambassador." The two policemen snapped smart salutes and I clambered up into the Landover showing everyone most of my thighs and probably my knickers. Stanley deposited my case into the open back of the long wheel-based vehicle containing an African youth who I hoped would guard my case. As Stanley got in, I asked, "Who is the young man in the back?"

He replied, "My son Morton. He is the turney boy."

I was then certain that I had gone through a looking glass. Life had taken on a strange turn of events. I expected at any moment that the phone would go to send me out into the Wiltshire countryside on a call to see a white rabbit. Instead, we met some giraffe and some zebra, then some fawn antelope. I looked them up in the guidebook, they were impala.

We bypassed Nairobi and went straight to the Veterinary Laboratories at Kabete. We stopped in front of the imposing door above which was written The Veterinary Department, Head Quarters (HQ). On the steps was standing a forlorn little boy aged about seven, crying his eyes out, holding an Alsatian almost bigger than him. I got out and said to the boy, "What a beautiful dog. What's her name?"

He answered with a sniff, "Beaver. We cannot find a home for her. We leave tonight and Dad says we will have to put her to sleep."

By now, Beaver was licking my hand. On impulse I said. "I'm a vet I love dogs. I will take her." The boy wrapped his arms round my legs, "Oh thank you, thank you. I will go and tell Mum." He dashed inside leaving me with my new dog. I opened the tailgate of the Landrover and said, "Get in." Beaver jumped in and greeted Morton. I asked Morton, "Will you look after her while I check in?"

"Yes, Madam." I followed Stanley into the building, and he said he would wait for me in the foyer. He suggested that I went up the stairs to The Director of Veterinary Services' (DVS) Office. I found the office which had a plaque and was at the top of the stairs. The door was ajar and there were men's voices coming from inside. I knocked and heard, "Come in."

I walked into the critical appraisal of three men. My heart sank. I thought I might as well have stayed in Wiltshire. However, the eldest who was in his sixties asked kindly, "How can we help you, young lady?"

I did not want to lie and say that I was Livingstone, so I rather foolishly said, "I am a vet. I have come to look after camels in Northern Kenya." There was an appalled silence. Then the youngest of the three said, "That's Lindstrom's UN/FAO project based in the Northern Frontier District (NFD). That's no place for a girl!"

I bristled, "I can assure you I am as good as any man." The older man who I righty assumed was the Director said, "I am sure you are. We will have to sort something out. We have got a beautiful Swedish built house for you which I am sure you will like. We were not expecting a young lady. We were expecting a Dr. Livingstone Fox."

I clarified the situation for them, "My middle name is Livingstone after my mother's family. My Christian name is Tanya." There was silence while they digested this information. The Director broke the silence, "I think what we all need is a good cup of coffee. Tanya, would you like to join us in the canteen. I can introduce you to some of our younger colleagues."

We all trooped down the stairs and across the drive to the canteen. I guessed that we were rather early, but I soon was sitting at a table with a cup of excellent coffee and piece of fruit cake. The Director introduced himself, "I am Terry Stokes, Michael Levin is my Deputy Director and John Adams is Assistant Director of Veterinary Services (ADVS) in charge of the field service which will include you." I knew immediately that he was the man which I had to convince that I could do the job. I smiled at John and said, "As I am a Kenyan Field Veterinary Officer (VO), do I report directly to you?"

John replied, "In essence yes. However, you will have to liaise with the provincial veterinary officers in charge of the provinces in which you are working, they are; Rift Valley Province, Eastern Province and North Eastern Province. There is no Provincial Veterinary Officer (PVO) for North Eastern Province. That province comes under Coast Province."

At the mention of the coast a vision of blue sea and palm trees flashed through my brain. I hoped I would like the guy in charge of the coast province. The Director interrupted my thoughts, "Your role Tanya will be slightly complicated as your salary and expenses are being paid by FAO." I laughed, "So I found out in Rome when they made me take off all my clothes except for my pants for a medical."

I did not need to look at any of the three men to know that they all had visions of me in the nude. The Director swallowed and continued, "Well I am sorry about that. You will be, what is going to be called, a Kenyan counterpart. You will be working closely with an FAO employee, Niels Lindstrom from Norway.

He is in charge of the project. He is up in Northern Kenya at the moment. He will be returning at the weekend. You will probably meet him as he is your next-door neighbour down at Lower Kabete. He is a charming man, with a lovely wife and two children.

Another senior looking man had entered the canteen. The Director said, "Are good, I would like you to meet Charles Shaw." The Director waved to this new guy, who came over. I jumped up. The Director rather formally said, "Charles, I would like you to meet Tanya Fox. She is going to be the Departments camel expert."

Charles shook my hand and said, "We certainly need an expert. There are probably ten million camels in the country, and we have not had anyone who knows anything about them since Jim Evans retired twenty years ago."

I may not be male, and have played rugby for Scotland, but I had done my homework. I ask, "Is that the Mr. Evans who has a Trypanosome named after him?"

Charles answered, "It is actually. He was a lovely man. Sadly, he died two years ago."

I responded, "I'm sorry to hear that. I would have valued his advice. I assume that you have as much a problem with *T. evansi* as the Sudanese."

Charles replied, "To be frank with you, Tanya. We don't know."

It was my turn to smile, "I can see I have got my work cut out."

Charles nodded, "I wonder if you would like to have dinner with me tonight to discuss a way forward?"

I answered, "I would like that very much."

Charles left. He had certainly upstaged these three men. I asked the Director, "Where does Mr. Shaw fit in?"

John answered for the Director, "He is my opposite number here at Kabete. He is the Assistant Director of Veterinary Services in charge of the laboratory services."

I had a lot to learn. I was going to have to manage all the politics of the department. I certainly had jumped into the fire. The three partners in the practice in Wiltshire had been very small beer compared with this lot. There was no way back for me now. I had to be the camel expert. I hoped Niels would be my salvation. We return the main building, back up the stairs to the Director's office. Then the Deputy Director of Veterinary Services (DDVS) leads me back down the stairs into another office and he finds the keys to my house. He kindly says, "Your house has good servants' quarters. I think Tanya that it would be good for you to employ someone to work for you. Your house will not have a washing machine. It has a log fire which you will need in the colder weather. We are at nearly six thousand feet here, so it can be a little chilly. Local labour is very inexpensive, would you like me and my wife to help you to recruit some one?"

I replied, "I will take your advice. Thank you for being so kind."

We walked out of the building. Morton and Stanley were chatting to an old man. The Deputy Director said, "Hello, Matua. Whose dog is this?"

Matua replied, "It was Mr. Richard's dog, Sir. This lady has said that she will take it on."

The DDVS looked at me inquiringly, I said, "A little boy reached out to my heart. His owners are leaving today.

The DDVS said. "It looks a good dog, Tanya. I don't think that you will regret getting a big dog. I had forgotten the Richards family were leaving." Then he turned to Matua, "Have you got a job Matua?"

Matua answered, "No Sir."

The DDVS Director asked him, "Would you look after this young lady."

Matua's face lit up. I liked his smile. "I would like such a job."

The DDVS turned to me. "I know Matua, he is a good man. You could always employ him for a month's trial to see how you get on. He is an excellent cook."

So, I had only been in the place three hours, and I had a house, a cook and a dog. Matua got in the back of the Landrover with Morton and Beaver. The Deputy Director who wanted me to call him Michael got in beside me in the front. We set off on the two-mile journey to Lower Kabete. My house was the end one, of three detached properties which each had gardens, a garage, a big shed and servant's quarters. They had been built with Swedish aid money. Niels and his family would be my next-door neighbours.

The property was very colourful with its own drive and big parking area at the back. There was a profusion of flowers. In front it had a patio and a lawn. There was a thin rose bed at the edge of the lawn with a dog proof fence behind which was a field containing some cattle which I found out later were experimental cattle used for trypanosomal research.

The inside of the house was very Scandinavian. There was a large living room at a lower level. There was a large open wood fire. This had an interesting feature which was a log storing area below the grate which would dry the wood. There was a dining room and a kitchen at ground level. All on the same level were three bedrooms and two bathrooms. Off the hall was a cloakroom. It was a house for a family, but I would be grateful for the space as I hoped friends and relatives would be coming out to stay. Kenya with its massive areas of wildlife national parks was an up-and-coming holiday destination.

The previous occupants had left curtains throughout together with some rugs on the beautiful wood floors. There were hard furnishings all in good condition. The mattresses and pillows looked clean and little used. All I would need to buy would be bedding. I would make do with my sleeping bag in the meantime. The previous occupants had left tableware and kitchen stuff.

As Michael had said there were no electrical appliances. There was a refrigerator which worked on paraffin. I wondered how that could possibly work. I looked at Matua. He smiled and took out a box of matches from his pocket. He moved the appliance out from the wall and lit the wick at the back before returning the fridge to its original position, saying "Soon cold." He obviously understood physics better than me.

I was delighted with the house and thanked Michael. Michael gave Matua some money and said something in Swahili. Then he turned to me and said, "Matua will buy you some basic supplies and fruit for breakfast. We will return to upper Kabete and get some lunch in the canteen. We can then sort out your transport unless you have brought a camel with you."

I knew I was going to get on well with Michael. I felt that I had really landed on my feet. Leaving Beaver with Matua we returned to main HQ. I was then shown to the office which Niels used. It was large. It was on the corner of the building on the upper floor with plenty of windows and therefore plenty of light. There were two desks and office chairs, together with filing cabinets and bookcases. The bookcases were empty, and I suspected the filing cabinets were as well.

On one wall was an enormous map of Kenya. There were red-headed pins in a cluster roughly in the centre above Mount Kenya. I asked Michael, "What do the red pins indicate?"

He replied, "I'm not certain, but I suspect they pinpoint clusters of camels. They are around Isiolo which is really the start of the Northern Frontier District or NFD as it is called. Niels is up there now. I think that he is trying to get a handle on the project. All I can say is I wish you the best of luck. Most people prefer the Highlands of Kenya which are much more populated with a good rainfall. The farming areas have an excellent climate. The NFD which is really the top part of the country is very dry, remote and desolate. Folk are frightened of it which is why John said it is not a place for a girl. You may be different. You make thrive in the NFD. I hope so."

I smiled at him, "I think what you are really saying is that the area is enjoyed by a few odd-balls and perhaps I am one of those."

He looked rather sheepish and nodded his head before saying, "To be honest I can't imagine why London recruited you."

Then realisation hit him, and he blurted out, "They thought you were a man and never interviewed you?" It was my turn to nod my head, "Please don't let on."

He laughed, "I never have had a daughter only two sons. I think you would have been the apple of my eye. Your secret is safe with me, but please take care, the NFD is very lawless. I will introduce you to a friend of mine, in fact, his wife and my wife are sisters. I'm sure he will guide you."

That is the first I had heard of Dick White who was a legend in the NFD and became my guide and mentor.

At lunch I was introduced to several laboratory vets and an interesting zoologist called Horatio Little. He like Dick White, but to a lesser extent, also became one of my mentors. I reflected as I tucked into my rice pudding that these senior men already had my respect which had been sadly lacking for my previous employers.

After lunch Michael took me to the transport yard and explained about drivers and vehicles. As I was the Kenyan counterpart for a UN/FAO project, things would be different for me from normal Kenyan Government Officers. Normally so called GK (Government of Kenya) officers were the only people allowed to drive and also to ride in GK vehicles. I was a GK officer and had those privileges. I also would be allowed to drive and ride in UN vehicles like the Landrover driven by Stanley this morning. The project had a second Landrover which was being used by Niels on his current safari. Its driver was Joseph and his turney boy was his son Zebedee. It all sounded rather incestuous. Niels also had a staff car which was for him, and his families use. I had a motorbike, a Triumph 500. I was delighted. Michael was very worried and made me promise to be careful. He said that Kenyan drivers were very inconsiderate. He stressed that the tarmac roads had potholes and the dirt or, so called murram roads, were treacherous when they were wet.

At Vet School I had briefly had a boyfriend who was an English student. He had had a motorbike. I had many fond memories of tearing along at breakneck speed with my arms tightly around his waist. I remember the shed attached to the garage at my new house. It would be an ideal place to keep the bike. Without further ado I invited Michael to take a spin with me on the bike to show me the area. I thought it was time that he had a mid-life crisis. Initially he put his arms tentatively around my waist. However rather than giving the whole of Kabete a view of my knickers as I was wearing a brown-coloured dress with a full mid-calf length skirt, I got him to put his hands on my thighs to keep my dress down. He seemed to enjoy this. We did a circuit which included an area of Nairobi called Westlands where I guessed I would be doing my shopping. When we arrived back at the HQ and he was getting off the bike he said, "Tanya, I really enjoyed that. I felt young again. I think you are just what the department required. London did well to recruit you."

I squeezed his hand, "Remember our secret."

He replied, "I will."

I got him to tell me how to get to Charles' house. I ask him what time I should aim to get there. He said, "Normally folk arrive after dark at about 7.30 pm. I think Charles will like the bike."

I gathered the normal office hours were 9 to 5, so soon I went on the bike down to my new home. Matua had been cleaning. The house smelt pleasantly of polish. Beaver gave me a greeting. Matua asked what time I would like supper. This was real luxury.

However, I told him that I had been invited out by Charles. His comment was, "He is a nice man you will have a good evening." It made me smile. Matua was old enough to be my grandfather he was obviously going to take care of me. Matua also took charge of Beaver as I saw he had bought a bag of dog food for her.

I commandeered the bedroom with the en suite bathroom and started to unpack my large rucksack. Matua came in and seemed worried that there were no sheets. I showed him my sleeping bag and said that I would buy some bed clothes tomorrow. He obviously understands a large amount of English. I made a mental note to learn to speak more Swahili. I also remembered reading in a guidebook that Kenyans also spoke their separate tribal language. I asked Matua which tribe he belonged to. He said that he was a Kikuyu which was the most numerous tribe. He said he also understood Stanley's tribal language which was Kipsigis. I ask him if he would help me with both languages as well as Swahili. This seemed to please him.

I was delighted that my bathroom had not only a bath but also a separate shower. I certainly needed a good shower and hair wash. I was amazed that while I was in the shower Matua had come in and taken all my dirty clothes away, as well bringing me a cup of tea. Wrapped in a towel I walked through to the kitchen to thank him. I got him to tell me what to say in Swahili and Kikuyu.

I am rather proud of my legs so I decided to wear a tight short skirt which might have been a little revealing as I got on to the motorbike but would not balloon up like a full skirt when I was on the move.

I was a little surprised as when I was brushing my hair, Matua came in to collect the empty teacup and saucer. He did not take it away, but he finished unpacking my rucksack. I did not stop him but watched as he put everything away, hanging up things which need hanging up. He had obviously been very well trained by a woman. I was delighted. I liked him. I was sure we would get on well. He took me to one of the built in cupboards. In it was a gun safe. He gave me the little flat key which was on a light chain. I put the chain which I guessed was stainless steel over my head so that the key was hidden under the collar of my blouse. He nodded approvingly.

Before I left to go out to dinner, I locked my small handbag which contained my English money and my passport into the safe. Back in England the Overseas Development Agency (ODA) had sent me various guides to working overseas. One advised me to open a local account in Nairobi to receive my local salary, but to keep my overseas top-up in the UK. I had been worrying about buying a vehicle, but I now realised that I would not have to. It was a real relief as I had never liked the thought of being in debt.

Charles was far from a typical bachelor. I guessed that there had never been a Mrs. Shaw, but that Charles liked female company. His house was spotlessly tidy, but he was a very relaxed host. I said, "I'm sorry not to bring you a bottle of wine. However, can we make a date for you to come to my house."

He answered, "I would like that a lot. Now what would you like to drink?"

I replied, "I gather there are four different local beers. I have not yet had a chance to sample any of them. Which one do you like?"

He smiled, "I'm a Tusker man."

I smiled back, "I would love a Tusker then."

I enjoyed it that I was given a pint mug and an ice-cold bottle of Tusker. He had the same. I took a sip. It tasted like the Indian Pale Ale my father drinks. I liked it and said so. Charles raised his glass to me. I did the same saying, "Cheers, here's to your good health."

He responded, "Welcome to Kenya. I like your motor bike."
I answered, "I'm delighted with it."
He asked, "Will you take me for a spin?"
I replied, "Come on then."

We put down our drinks and like a couple of kids almost ran outside. That set the tone for the evening. It was great fun. I found him very interesting. He was excellent company and very young at heart. The difference between him and my old employers was very marked. He was constantly asking for my views, and we had some lively discussions. His cook looked like Stanley. I was very bold and asked him if he was a Kipsigis. He replied that he was. He beamed when I attempted to greet him in his tribal language, having remembered what Matua had told me. Of course, he knew Stanley. I said how pleased I had been that he had been at the airport to meet me.

His cooking was good. His name was Kipchoge. I put my head into the kitchen to say goodbye as I was leaving. Charles seemed to like this and as he shook me by the hand, he said, "You will go a long way in this country Tanya."

I had been careful to stick to only two bottles of beer. I did not want to fall off the bike on the way home. I knew it was only two miles, but I remembered my promise to Michael.

I was delighted to find a long heavy torch on my desk in the morning with a note from Charles. It read. 'I saw your bike had saddlebags. I would keep this near you when you are out. It might be useful if you breakdown. I had a spare one.'

I immediately rang him on the internal line to thank him and confirm our date for two evening's time. I had no sooner put the phone down when Michael knocked on the door. He had brought a file with him. He showed me how the government filing system worked. It was new to me and seemed very efficient. I asked, "Do I start looking at the files which come into the office?"

He replied, "I would. Initially you ought to run them by Niels but soon you will need to complete a monthly report to The Veterinary Department. Niels will make a similar report to FAO. You could ask the registry to let you have his reports. He only started three months ago so it won't be arduous."

Chapter 4

Michael was right. Niels had done very little except to start a census of all the camels in Kenya. As I had nothing else to do, I decided to see what equipment the project had got. I thought Stanley would know. I found him and Morton at the transport yard. They did not know what equipment FAO had supplied, but they did know there were some large crates in a storeroom which had been allocated to the project. Armed with three jemmies we went to investigate. The storeroom was enormous. It was really a small hanger. I was surprised that these large crates had been allowed into the country without being opened by customs, until I remembered that FAO was part of the UN and their vehicles had special status and were exempt from customs duty.

The first crate we tackled was full of laboratory equipment. Leaving Stanley and Morton to tackle the opening of another crate, I decided to get some laboratory space for us. I went to see Charles. He smiled when I went into his office, after I had knocked on the door, "You look like a girl on a mission. How can I help you?" I looked down at my clothes. They were already filthy, covered in red dust.

I said, "Oh dear I spent my whole life dirty in practice in the UK. A change of continent has not altered me. I need some laboratory space."

He laughed, "I am ahead of you. I have earmarked the old diagnostic lab to your project. We now have a full-blown diagnostic unit. FAO have recruited a laboratory technician. I have his file here. He passed it over to me. It contained his CV. Without thinking I said when I saw his small photo, "He is quite good looking."

Charles chuckled, "If you read on, He has a young wife."

I laughed, "I was only making an idle comment. Anyhow I have a boyfriend."

Charles looked surprised, I continued, "I took him on a night-time adventure last night on my motorbike. I have already been reprimanded by the Director."

He then realised that I was teasing him. He got up, "Come on I will show you the small lab." He took some keys off a series of hooks on a board by the door.

The lab had fitted benches and cupboards. Otherwise, someone had stripped the room bare. Charles said, "Sadly the diagnostic unit have taken all their equipment. However there it is. He handed me the keys. I said, "I don't mind that it is empty. FAO have sent a whole crate of equipment. I hope I won't have upset anyone. I have got Stanley and Morton to open the crates."

He was very reassuring, "The Kabete lab is a very friendly place. Everyone mucks in. They are more regimented in the field. The Provincial Veterinary Officers are rather protective of their provinces."

I replied, "I rather gathered that from John Adams. I will have to tread carefully, as I understand I will be operating in four provinces."

It was his turn to tease me, "I'm sure your cheeky smile will help!" I punched him playfully on the chest as I took the keys.

I soon got Stanley and Morton to help me move the lab equipment to our laboratory, after we had swept the floor and dusted the shelves. We checked everything off on the inventory.

We then set about opening the biggest crate. To my amazement the inventory said that it was a microlight. What a find. I had my own air transport. I looked down the list of the stuff which was included. There were four pieces of aluminium listed as camera brackets. Obviously, this had been purchased by FAO to help the project to carry out the census of the camels which poor Niels was laboriously carrying out on the ground. We did not take anything out of the crate but left everything packed up. We opened a smaller yet heavy crate which contained the engine. Another small crate yielded the camera.

I asked Stanley and Morton not to tell anyone else. I wanted to make sure that I was going to be the pilot. I went back to the office and looked in the yellow pages. There was no mention of anyone who sold or rented out microlights. I got on my bike and roared into Nairobi. I soon found the prestigious McMillan library guarded by two imposing stone lions.

The elderly librarian, Anthony Banks was intrigued by my request for information about microlights. His research led us to gyrocopters. He helped me to find a reference in The Encyclopaedia Britannica. We read that they had been invented by a Spaniard in the 1920s. Sadly he could find no reference to a microlight. I obviously had something rather revolutionary. Anthony took a shine to me. He invited me to lunch at The New Stanley Hotel nearby. This is a famous hotel often called the Thorn Tree as there is a tree in the sitting area outside of the hotel. Anthony said he always went there on a Friday as that day of the week they had a marvellous smorgasbord. He was right it was magnificent. We both tucked in. We were soon joined by a middle-aged man who was an acquaintance of Anthony's. Anthony introduced us. His name was Dick White. I had heard that name before, but I could not remember when. It was only, when he said that he always tried to get back from his safaris by Friday lunch time, because he so enjoyed this meal that I remembered who he was. He was Michael's brother-in-law. Michael had described him as a legend in the NFD. I said, "Mr. White, I have so wanted to meet you. I'm going to be working with camels in the NFD. Your brother-in-law has said I should meet you as you could help me." His face lit up, "I will be delighted. I spend most of my time up in the NFD. I am going up to buy cattle in Moyale on Monday. Would you like to join me. I would be glad of the company."

I replied, "That would be magic. I have a Landrover. What kit should I bring?"

He answered, "I will be bringing my cook, so you don't need to worry about food. What do you like to drink?"

I replied, "Beer."

He smiled, "Very wise, it can get hot. If you can bring a cold box with some beer that would be excellent. Also, if you can bring a tent with a mosquito net and a camp bed that would be good. Are you taking anything for Malaria?"

I nodded, "Yes I was told to take two Paludrine every day."

Dick suggested, "A chair and table would be helpful. As would a Tilly Light. Of course, you should bring plenty of Jerry cans of water and petrol. I like to leave in the cool of the morning. Shall we meet here at 6.00 am."

I answered. "I will be here. Can I bring my dog?"

He replied, "Certainly. If you bring a driver, we will get the two drivers to go together. You can drive me and then we can chat."

I was so excited that I forgot all about the microlight.

So, I spent the afternoon doing some more unpacking. I managed to find all the camping equipment that I needed. There were metal and plastic jerrycans. I got Morton to fill the plastic ones with water. Luckily Stanley knew all about buying the petrol. If we had been using a GK Landrover we would have had to get forms in triplicate from the administration office called Local Purchase Orders (LPOs). However, the Landrover which I was going to be taking had red numberplates and belonged to the FAO. This vehicle like my motorbike had to be filled up using different forms. Stanley had a handle on the whole situation. He was meticulous when it came to packing up the vehicle. I was relying on him to ensure that nothing would get broken. Special attention was paid to the Tilly light.

Matua and Stanley seemed to get on well together, so they liaised regarding the food and the beer. Stanley was delighted to go on safari because he would be paid a living out allowance which was particularly generous as we were going to the NFD. Morton would also get an allowance.

After work I called in to introduce myself to the Lindstrom's. Niels was still away but would hopefully get back in the evening. His wife was a delightful woman called Elisabeth and her two daughters were Trudi and Gretel. They made a big fuss of Beaver and insisted on taking her for a walk.

Matua cooked an excellent meal for Charles and me. He had brought a bottle of red wine which the two of us polished off. I was quite merry as I got into bed. I had bought some sheets and pillowcases, so I was in a proper bed. Matua had said that he would put my sleeping bag ready to go on safari.

How my life had changed. Matua woke me with a cup of tea. I felt like royalty. As I got dressed, I saw that all my clothes had been beautifully washed and ironed. He made me a good breakfast. I had no trouble getting to work on time. Niels arrived soon after me. He was rather serious and taciturn, but he seemed a very kind man. They say opposites attract each other. Elisabeth was a very bubbly character. I reflected that now I had left the practice in UK you might well term me bubbly.

Niels seemed to respond to my enthusiasm. He was pleased that I had arranged a safari so soon. He had set his heart on getting more pins in our map. However, he said that he was lonely away from his family, if I was happy to go on safari, he said he would be delighted to let me get on with the census. I took him to see the microlight having begged him not to tell anyone else. He was intrigued. He could easily see the advantages of carrying out the census by air. He also realised that I was an adventurist. As a family man he had no desire to risk his neck travelling in what he thought of as a flying bedstead.

I realised that Niels was very much an administration/laboratory vet. He was pleased that a lab technician was coming to join us. He would be pleased to hand over all the sampling which needed to be done over to me. Although we had yet to unpack some of the crates, I had seen that there was an enormous number of sample bottles. There were also two very large deep freezes. I could start collecting samples which we could store in the deep freeze to await the arrival of the laboratory technician.

Niels spoke perfect English like the rest of his family. He was happy to try and find some textbooks in English on camels. He laughed and said there were certainly no Norwegian textbooks on camels, but he had seen two large tomes on reindeer.

It seemed as if there was often a meeting at a club called the Kabete Club on Saturday morning at noon when everyone stopped work for the weekend. Niels said that he had joined as a member because he was a keen golfer. He took me along. I recognised several faces from the canteen. I enjoy playing tennis and squash. I was delighted there were two courts for both sports. I was soon proposed as a member. The golf course was beautiful. I wondered if I might have a go at playing. I was told that there were many members of the club who lived locally but were not part of the Veterinary Laboratory staff. I liked the idea of meeting other people. I was delighted that because I worked for the Veterinary Laboratory my membership was free.

In the afternoon I took Beaver for a long walk. The countryside was very different from England. The birdlife was spectacular. I was glad I had brought a pair of binoculars with me. I would need to get a bird book.

I mentioned this to Michael when I arrived for dinner. He immediately lent me a good guide to the birds of east Africa. He also lent me a book on the history of the country which contained some interesting old photographs. His wife, Judy was very motherly. I don't think she approved of my motorbike and certainly not my short skirt. It made me smile as I often caught Michael looking at my legs.

I enjoyed my supper. I learnt a large amount about the area known as Kabete. The Government Veterinary Office was just one of a number of other educational establishments. There was the East African Trypanosome Research Organisation (EATRO) which as the name suggests does research on the protozoans which infect man and animals as well as the main vector, the Tsetse fly. Next door was the East African Virus Research Organisation (EAVRO). There were plans for a Veterinary School to produce home grown vets and plans for an Animal Health and Industrial Training Institute (AHITI) which would train veterinary technicians which were called veterinary scouts. Apparently, I would have the help of veterinary scouts throughout the NFD.

Although it was chilly early in the morning at Kabete it was never really cold. I loved being woken by a cup of tea brought to my bedside in the morning. It was a struggle, but we made it with two minutes to spare at the New Stanley. Dick and his staff were already there, but he promised me that they had not been waiting long. I moved out of my Landrover and took over driving Dick. He gave me very relaxed directions. I was wearing shorts, so my legs got more than a passing glance.

We had good tarmac for the first hundred miles which took us past Thika. It was still dark so I could not see the massive acreage of pineapples grown by Delmonte's. The dawn came soon. Mount Kenya with its two peaks, Batian and Nelion which are over seventeen thousand feet were hidden in the morning cloud on our right. Dick said that if I was lucky, we might see the top later in the morning. On our left were the Aberdare range of hills, well really, they were mountains as they were over thirteen thousand feet above sea level.

We stopped in Nanyuki at The Nanyuki Sports Club for a hearty breakfast. Dick proposed me for membership. He said it was considerably cheaper than the clubs around Nairobi and that there was a scheme of reciprocation so that I could use their facilities. While we were eating our breakfast. The two drivers filled up with fuel and Morton took Beaver for a walk.

Ten miles out of Nanyuki we reached Timau which was the end of the tarmac and the good farming land. Looking north I could see the endless miles of the NFD stretching out before me. Dick looked behind but said that the mountain was still in cloud. We started to lose altitude from seven thousand to three thousand feet. We were heading for the hot country. Our target for a fuel stop was Isiolo. Here I saw my first camel. I told Dick about the microlight.

He said, "I think that you are totally crazy, but I hope that you will take me up in it. There is a guy called Percy Gibbons in Nyeri which we passed to our left earlier. He had one. He flew it for some time but managed to write it off coming into land on his ranch. I will introduce you to him. I am sure he will teach you to fly the thing. He is not the sharpest tool in the shed, so you ought to be able to manage!"

After filling up in Isiolo where, to my delight there were camels all over the place. We went on the short distance to the police post at Archer's Post. Dick was obviously well known to the askaris, but we had to sign in as we officially were entering the NFD. Immediately past the barrier was a long concrete bridge which crossed the Ewaso Nyiro River. This river never reaches the sea but is lost in the Lorain Swamps at a place called Muddo Gashi. Dick pointed out a turning on our right to Muddo Gashi which ultimately went to Mandera. He promised to take me there, as it was the most northerly point of the country where Kenya met with Ethiopia and Somalia.

In front of us was a large sugar loaf rock, called Lolokwi. I stopped to take a picture. The place was deserted and very hot. Stanley and Zac, Dick's driver took off the side windows of the Landrovers to let more air in. I asked Dick, "Will anyone mind if I take off some clothes?" He raised his eyebrows. I laughed, "I have got my bikini on!"

Dick with a wry smile said, "What a shame. I imagine you want to get a tan. You will have to be careful with your shoulders as the sun will burn you unless you take it slowly. I suggest you put on a safari hat like me to protect your head and face."

I took his advice. He did some driving so that my right arm did not get browner than my left arm which was kind. I think he was impressed how well I took a tan.

I got him to tell me what his job was. He was the head of the Livestock Marketing Division (LMD). It was part of the Veterinary Department but got separate finance. He controlled its one-line vote. He explained this to me. The Veterinary Department like other Government Departments got funds for recurrent running expenses, like running of vehicles, salaries, repairing building, uniforms etc. They also got development expenses which were for capital expenses. The LMD just got a lump sum, a so-called one-line vote which could be spent at his discretion. It was large and was to be spent on buying cattle. The LMD bought these cattle from traders mainly Arabs who were shop owners in the NFD. The Veterinary Department vaccinated them against Rinderpest and blood tested them against Contagious Bovine Pleural Pneumonia (CBPP), then the LMD brought them south through a series of holding grounds. Eventually they sold them to ranchers to fatten or grow on to be breeding stock. The money circulated. It was a money earner for the treasury, and it helped the pastoral people who lived in the NFD to get money to buy them food and consumer goods.

It sounded a very good idea. I asked, "Could the LMD buy camels?"

He replied certainly, "I understood that is what FAO are interested in. I imagine that they have plans to export camels to the Middle East. The difficulties are that no one knows really what diseases they may get. There have been some disasters in the past where hundreds of camels have died."

I laughed, "I really have got to get down to some real veterinary work. I see now why we need to count the numbers and find out what causes them to die."

Dick laughed, "Of course you also have got to get a tan."

I replied, "Naturally, just to look pretty for you. I have noticed that you have been studying my legs."

He laughed, "I am delighted that now there is more of your anatomy on display."

We ground on driving, on the dusty road. We only saw two lorries the whole day. They were full of people presumably coming to Isiolo. I was filthy when we eventually drew to a halt under some tall trees at a place called Laisamis. There was nothing at Laisamis except a sand lugger with a few greenish pools of water. Dick told me that we would camp under these trees well away from the lugger which harboured sand flies. These gave horrible itchy bites. They were small enough to get through mosquito netting. They laid their eggs in moist sand in the lugger.

It was 4.00 pm so there was at least two hours of day light left. We all set about making camp. There were six of us. Dick's driver was called Zak and his cook was a man originally from Ethiopia called Marco. It did not seem to matter that I was dressed only in my bikini and my gym shoes which I gathered were called takkis. Two tables were put up under the trees with six chairs. Zebedee got a small gas stove lit and made us all mugs of tea. Morton collected dry wood and made a fire. He filled a blackened metal bucket with water which was put beside the fire. Zak helped Dick to put up his tent which I gather was a type of tent called a 'Nandi'. Mine was the same and Stanley helped me. You could just stand in the tent. It was long enough to erect the six-foot camp bed. It had windows with sewn-in mosquito netting and a flap door. The bed had a mattress. I found my pillow and sleeping bag. Zak and Marco were going to sleep in the back of one Landrover. Stanley and Morton were going to sleep in the other. Tilly lamps were found. Marco had a third table for his cooking which was going to be done partly on the fire and partly on the stove. A small paraffin fridge was lit. A canvas basin was set up and a canvas bag with a rose at the bottom was pulled up on to a branch of a tree.

Dick had the first shower. It was still light, so I just looked the other way. The other men folk all followed. The rapid dusk was falling when I took my shower. It definitely was not dark, so I gave them all a good view. I was not too fussed. Dick had obviously had a look as he remarked, "You are amazing. You have got tan marks already." I just smiled. I knew I would not say anything to Helen his wife when I met her. I had already met her sister, Judy who was Michael's wife.

It was totally dark by the time we ate dinner. The beautiful steaks were just as I like, rare. There were green beans and boiled potatoes with them. The meal was washed down with cold beers. Pudding was juicy pineapples, followed by black coffee and African cream liqueur. We could have been dining in the Ritz. I helped Marco with the washing up while the others collected more wood.

All this time Beaver had rested under a tree. Dick and I took him for a walk with our torches after the meal. It was delightfully scary in the African night walking away from the light of the fire. I was glad Beaver made no attempt to run off. Dick had a pee and I squatted down not far from him. He explained that if I wanted a poo, I should not go far away. I should take some loo-roll, matches and a machete called a panga. I should dig a small hole do my business, use the loo-roll, set light to the paper, and cover the hole in. It was all very simple and hygienic.

I slept well. Beaver joined me in the tent. In the morning there was more tea. Toast was made on a metal frame over the fire. There was marmalade or honey. Butter was from a wide necked thermos. There was also bacon and scrambled eggs. We then packed up the camp. However, we had to do that with some speed as we were going to shoot our supper. We drove to the lugger. Dick got out his shot gun. We were only just in time. Apparently, you could set your clock by the arrival of the sand grouse. They were flying in for the water. They stored it in the feathers on their legs before flying home to their nests which could be tens of miles away in the dry country.

It was great shooting. Dick shot several brace. Then lending me his settler jacket to protect my shoulder from the kick he gave me a go. I had done some clay pigeon shooting before on the farm at home in the UK. I was no way near as good as him, but I was pleased that I managed to hit three. Suddenly the birds stopped coming. That was it. Dick told me there was a species which flew in, in the evenings, but their timing was not nearly so reliable. The dead birds were hung by their necks in the back of the Landrover to cool off in the breeze.

I was, not only pleased with the shooting, but also, I was delighted that Beaver had not been frightened by the gun shots. The retrieving of the birds was easy as the bush was not thick and most of the birds fell in the sand of the lugger.

We set off north to do the hundred miles to reach Marsabit mountain which was five thousand feet high in the middle of the dessert. Before we reached Marsabit we had to drive through two more sand luggers. These were much wider and were impassable in the rainy season. However, in four-wheel drive, we got the Landrovers through.

Initially Marsabit was just a blue haze in the distance. Slowly it took shape. It was a game reserve and was home to a very famous elephant called Ahmed. He was very old and had enormous tusks which were said to weigh over a hundred pounds each. They dragged in the ground, as he walked. He was guarded by two younger elephants. The three of them were guarded by game rangers working on shifts.

I was interested to see an airstrip beside the road at the bottom of the mountain. Dick told me that it had been made as the airstrip up near Marsabit town was often in cloud. Pilots could land safely on this lower strip and wait for the cloud to clear, or they could walk or get transport up to the town. We started up the road to the town. We left the acacia scrub behind and entered a green world. First it was grassland and then as we got higher it turned into forest. I hoped to see a bongo which is a very rare antelope, but Dick told me that he had never been lucky. The forest also was meant to contain some greater kudu, but Dick was certain from talking to the game rangers that they were no longer present on the mountain. Because the area was so remote and visitors always came in by air, there were no park gates, but I guessed that we had reached the park as we saw two rangers walking with their rifles down the road towards us.

Dick chatted to them in Swahili. I longed to understand the language. They were just about to enter the forest to relieve their companions who guarded the three elephants. Dick had persuaded them to let us follow them.

The two drivers and Marco and Morton continued in the vehicles into town to fill up with fuel, water, and provisions. I quickly changed from my shorts into my jeans much to Dick's amusement. I wanted to avoid getting my legs scratched. It was so exciting to be following the rangers into the forest. Soon we came across piles of elephant dung which was still steaming. I hardly dared to breath. Our guides did not speak when we met their colleagues. We were near enough to the elephants in the thick bush to reach out and touch them. There was a continuous noise of their teeth grinding and their tummies rumbling. I had no way of knowing which elephant was Ahmed until a ranger touched my arm and pointed to the ground. There were the tell-tale tracks of his tusks making furrows in the soil. It was a magical experience, and I was sorry to leave.

Our new guides who were returning to Marsabit, took us on a more direct path. We went by an algae covered lake called 'Lake Paradise' Dick teased me saying he would look the other way if I wanted to take my clothes off and have a swim. There was no way I was going in the water. The lake was only two hundred yards from the road and so we soon found the others by the single petrol station. Marco had managed to buy some fresh goat meat and cabbage for supper. Sadly, there was no bread, butter, or milk available.

Once again, we set off heading north. We were soon descending, and it got hot very quickly as the day was warming up. Once again, I stripped off into my bikini. We were back into desert-like conditions. In fact, to our left was The Chalabis Desert where there was no vegetation at all. We had one hundred and sixty miles to reach Moyale.

It was a hot dusty journey. Often, I had to drop into four-wheel drive and go into low range to get through the deep sand. It was well into the afternoon when we could see the Ethiopian escarpment in the distance. As we approached, the road turned to our right and we came towards the escarpment at an angle. Dick had a favourite group of trees for our camp beside the airstrip. There were a few poor looking cattle grazing at the other end of the runway.

Leaving the others to set up camp, Dick and I drove up the escarpment following a rough, rocky road which was barely more than a track. Eventually we arrived at the border town of Moyale which was right on the edge of the escarpment. The NFD stretched away to the south but even with binoculars I could not see Marsabit.

There was one petrol station where we stopped to fill up. There were no provisions to be bought. According to the Arab shop owner, Kenyans went over to buy food in Ethiopia as it was cheaper. Dick advised me not to go into Ethiopia unless I had been officially invited as I would be likely to be locked up. It would have been different if I had brought my passport. I wondered also if it would have been better if I had been wearing more clothes. It felt odd in a garage just wearing a bikini.

We went to the District Officer's Office. The DO was a tall Boran man. He had received word on the radio from the DC in Marsabit. Dick and I had blotted our copy book as we had forgotten to call to see the DC and the District Livestock Officer (DLO). There was just an old veterinary scout who told us that word had been sent out and so he expected cattle to arrive in the evening or tomorrow morning. We returned to our camp just as darkness descended.

Dick berated himself for not following the protocol, but neither of us wanted to return all the way to Marsabit. The camp was very welcoming, with the fire and the tilly lamps lit. I was surprised that there was no one about but pleased to have a shower. Marco's sand grouse stew which was just their breasts with onions, carrots and herbs was very tasty. Pudding was rice pudding and jam, followed by the sweet African Cream liqueur.

I slept well with Beaver to guard me. I was tired from all the travelling and the two early starts. Dick promised me a lie in on the following morning. I did sleep later but once the sun was properly up, I got dressed. Marco must have heard me as he brought me a cup of tea. Breakfast was going to be porridge and honey.

Over breakfast, Dick and I discussed communications or really the lack of them. We both agreed that we needed radios. He got a map. We decided that every DLO to the east of Lake Rudolf would need one together with certain veterinary scouts at the holding grounds and other key spots like here at Moyale and Garsen where a ferry crossed the Tana River.

Dick thought we could get the funds from several sources: his LMD vote, my project funds and from the veterinary department. We agreed to tackle the problem when we returned to civilisation. I took Beaver for a long walk eastwards on a cattle trail at the bottom of the escarpment. I returned on another path on the slope of the escarpment. I was careful. I did not want to stray into Ethiopia and cause an international incident. At one point I got a better view of the plain below me. It was empty of cattle. Sadly, I thought that we had had a wasted journey regarding buying cattle, but I had had a marvellous debut trip into the NFD, and I had seen the backside of Ahmed!

We had a relaxing lunch and afternoon. At teatime we had good news. Five Arab traders arrived to see Dick. They promised that their cattle would arrive before dusk. They would keep them guarded but let them graze at the bottom of the escarpment. When they left, we had a beer to celebrate and when it was dark, we had showers.

The cattle did arrive. There were approximately two thousand. I knew Dick had been hoping for more. The quality was not nearly as good as he had hoped for. He reckoned he could not buy at least ten percent of them, mainly old cows, because they would not be fit enough to make the trip down south. I warned him that it looked like none of them had been vaccinated against Rinderpest as they did not have the Z brand on their rumps. I was sure the Veterinary Department would want them to be vaccinated before they set off. I had seen a boma and a long cattle race on my walk so at least there were facilities available.

I stood and watched the cattle. I did not see any with respiratory distress so hopefully any cattle which were bought would blood test negative for CBPP.

Dick had asked the traders about camels. I had not seen any on my walk. They said there were camels in quite large numbers along the escarpment. They did not report any sickness. They thought that the owners would be happy for me to blood test them provided I was able to come to them rather than ask them to trek the camels to a certain place. I thought that was an encouraging start. The garage owner at Marsabit had already told me that there were camels on the mountain. I hoped they would be happy to let me blood test them if I were to follow them about. I understood from Dick that I would not need a race or a crush, as the camels were trained to Kush at a very early age. Obviously, I would need to blood test a whole range of age groups from as large an area as possible.

I was interested in the buying process. There was a considerable amount of trust on both sides. The traders presented them in quite small, age and sex grouped, mobs which Dick recorded for each owner. The traders accepted that Dick could not buy animals which were not strong enough to make the trek south. These they would slaughter locally to be sold as meat for the local populous in small numbers according to demand.

There was a lot of haggling about the price particularly at the beginning. Dick knew what he could get for the finished product, but he had to factor in the costs of getting the animals down to the holding grounds near to the ranches. He had to estimate the number of deaths. At least with cattle, unlike me with camels he had some idea what diseases he was up against. He had told me that there was no tickborne disease in the NFD and there were very few areas where the dreaded tsetse flies which spread trypanosomiasis, lived. I knew there was no human trypanosomiasis in Kenya except around Lake Victoria. However, I also knew that there are at least three strains of trypanosomes which could cause acute and chronic disease in cattle. I suspected they would also cause disease in camels, but no one was certain. It was surprising that game animals were not affected although it was a widely held belief that they harboured the protozoan parasites. It was known that all three of the stains which affected cattle, affected horses and to some extent donkeys. They were certainly lethal but there was some evidence that donkeys had some resistance. I had seen large numbers of donkeys in the Kenyan highlands on the journey up to Nanyuki. There had been a lot in Isiolo and on Marsabit mountain.

The buying of cattle ceased towards the middle of the day. Dick hoped that more would be presented, when the heat of the day had passed. He was unlucky. He had only managed to buy one thousand, two hundred and forty animals. This was not very good news as the cost of trekking to some extent was more expensive with smaller numbers. Dick had told me that he liked to have three herdsmen per hundred head of cattle so that cost was linked to numbers. However, the number of lorries was static in that he would need two for a thousand head and still only two for five thousand head. The price had been agreed except he was not duty bound to buy any animals which tested positive for CBPP, but like me he did not think this was a problem. He did tell me that CBPP was one of the reasons that the government had little success in buying cattle in Masailand. He could not tell me why the Masai did not like selling any cattle and yet the members of the Samburu and the Rendile tribes which were closely related to them in the NFD were more amenable to selling their cattle.

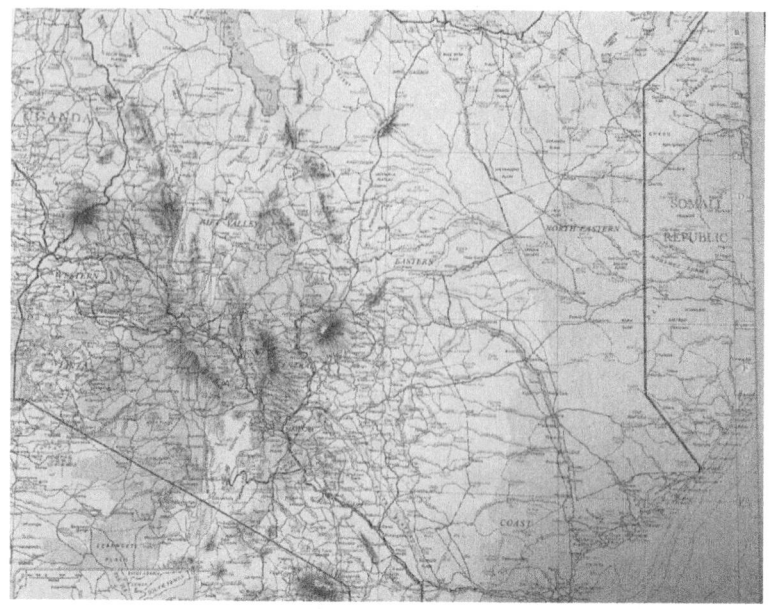

Map of Kenya showing altitude. Green is sea level up to 656 feet. Then the ground rises to white which is above 13,123 feet.

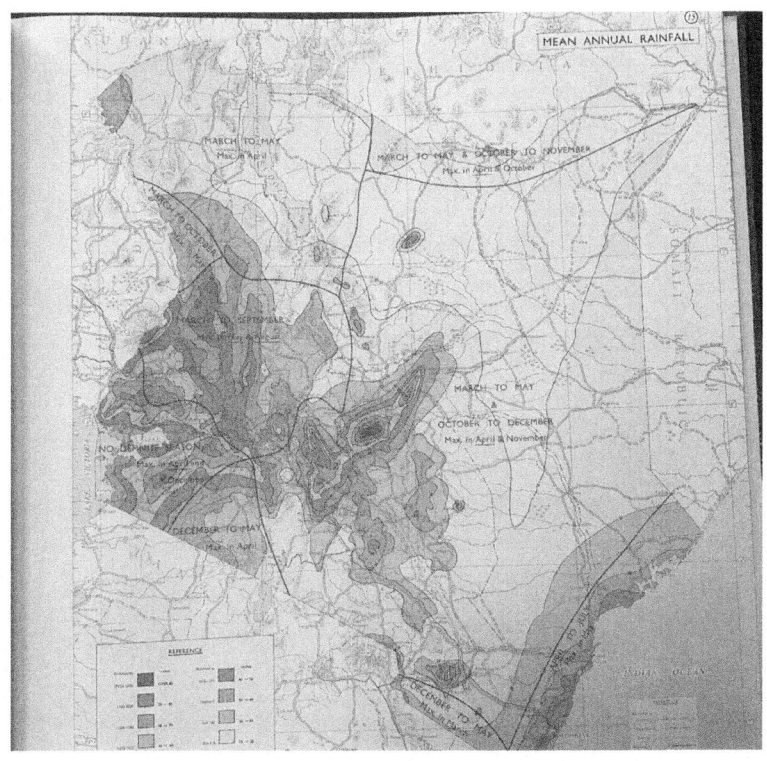

Map of Kenya showing the mean annual rainfall. Turquoise is over 80 inches per year down to light yellow which is below 10 inches a year.

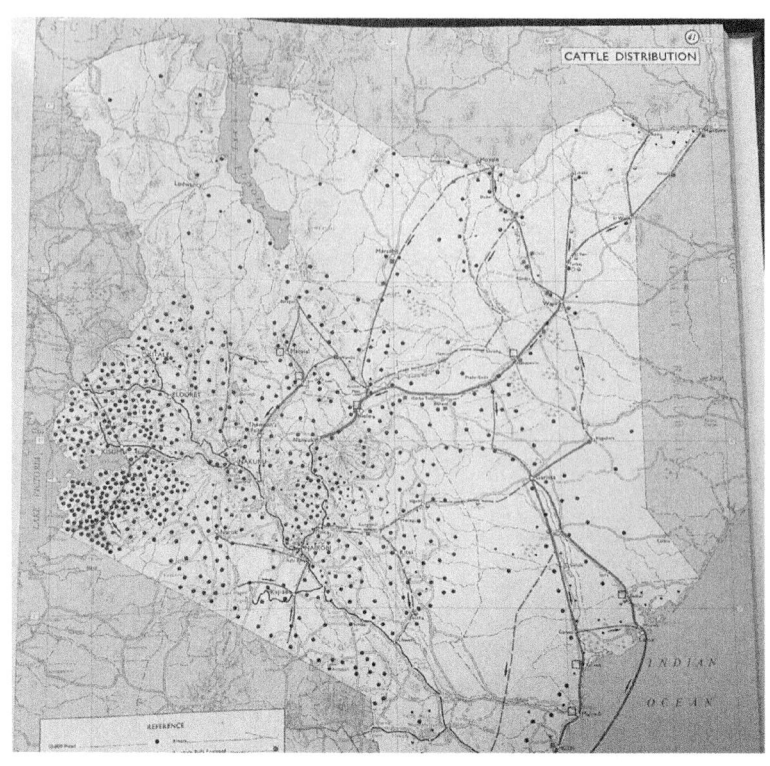

Map of Kenya showing cattle distribution. A large black dot indicates 10,000 head. A small dot indicates 1,000.

Chapter 5

In the morning we were on our way home again. This time we remembered to call into the district offices in Marsabit to see the DC and the DLO. I learnt that Marsabit was a district in the Eastern Region. At some stage I would have to visit the PVO Eastern in Machakos.

It was a dusty tiring journey. The two drivers and Morton elected to stay on the LMD holding ground at Isiolo. They had friends there and perhaps more importantly they would receive another night's living out allowance. Dick, Marco and I pressed on as it was Saturday, and we valued the rest day on Sunday. I dropped off Dick and Marco in Nairobi after 1.00 am. Dick was worried that I still had the five miles to go to get to Lower Kabete. I reassured him that I would be fine particularly as I had Beaver with me. Indeed, I was, as surprisingly I had got my second wind. I had often found at student balls that I was wilting at midnight, but somehow got a boost of energy in the early hours of the morning.

Beaver knew she was home as we swung into my drive. I just locked everything except my clothes bag in the Landrover as I knew I had Sunday to myself. We really did not make any noise, but Matua surprised me as I came out of the shower naked. I was more embarrassed than he was. He had two wives, so my body was obviously nothing to write home about. He had brought me a mug of hot chocolate and a glass of African Cream. Both were like nectar. I slept like a log and was amazed to find a hot cup of tea on my bedside table to wake me. He had unpacked my bag and taken all my clothes away for washing. I planned to have a lazy day at home. However, I had two visitors, Trudi, and Gretel.

They had come round to ask me to a bar-B-Que that evening and if they could take Beaver for a walk.

I was pleased that I could make Matua have the rest of the day off. He tried to protest saying that with me being on safari he had had most of the week off. I knew that was rubbish as the house was spotless.

I decided to forgo lunch as the bar-B-Q was scheduled for 4.00 pm to make the most of the daylight and so the children could get to bed for school the following day. There was another Scandinavian family at the bar-B-Q. They were Swedes and lived in the house the other side of the Lindstrom's. They were Rune and Margit they also had two daughters, Astrid, and Britta. The four girls were close friends. Rune was a vet and oversaw the Central Artificial Insemination Station (CAIS) which was just across the road. He was an interesting man. Kenya had pioneered AI in cattle in the 1930's. The government had seen a need to upgrade the local zebu cattle so that the progeny would produce more milk. Also, I had be unaware that there was a breeding disease in Kenya called 'Epivag'. All other breeding diseases in cattle affected the fertility of the cow. 'Epivag' affected the epididymis of the bull and made him infertile and very sore. Using AI rather than natural service prevented the spread of breeding disease.

It was an enjoyable evening. I think they all were surprised that I had spent the week in the NFD and had travelled to the very north of the country.

When I got to office in the morning, I started to investigate the purchase of long wave radios. It seemed that they could run off a car battery so that they were not dependent on an electricity supply. As a government department we would have no problem getting licences for them after we had been granted a frequency. They would need an aerial ten metres long which would need to be at least ten metres off the ground. Range would not be a problem as they could transmit for a thousand miles. Niels said he would be happy to recommend that the project purchase ten of them. Hopefully FAO would pay. I rang Dick. He said that he could find funds to pay for five. I went along to Michael's office. He did not need much feminine charm before he agreed to pay for a further five.

My next project was to get further maps to show us where in the country there were diseases which existed which would affect camels. I was delighted that as we were a government department, we could get them free from the Directory of Surveys. I got on my motorbike and took a trip into Nairobi to locate the office of the Director of Surveys. It was in Government Road. They were most helpful. I came back with a beautiful large, red-bound atlas and two large wall maps showing the distribution of tsetse flies and ticks both of which I thought would spread disease in camels.

Niels and I studied them. Overall, the NFD was free of tsetse flies except towards the coast and along the Tana River. There had been a species called *Glossina longipennis,* which made me giggle. It had been recorded in two small areas, one to the east of Marsabit and another to the east of Moyale.

We would have to be careful if we ever brought camels to the coast. There were several species of tsetse flies recorded in Tsavo Game Park, both East and West. I could see how these vast parks had been made into game parks. No pastoral people could live there as their cattle would die.

What we did not know was where the biting flies which spread *Trypanosoma evansi* lived. One reference book suggested that they only occurred in damp areas so that the majority of the NFD would be free. What we could not find out was whether the sand luggers would be a breeding ground for these biting flies.

I did know that camels were affected by a disease spread by ticks called Heart Water which was caused by a bacterium. Luckily there were very few recordings of ticks in the NFD. What of course we did not know was whether they did not exist or whether they just had not been recorded. I was a little bit despondent when I came home after work. There was so much that I needed to find out.

I had just eaten my supper when the telephone rang. In the UK my heart would stop as I would expect a call to go out in the cold. Here it was not cold, and any contact was very welcome. The caller said, "You won't know who I am, but my name is Percy Gibbons."

I replied, "I remember your name. Dick White told me that you farm near Nyeri and used to own a microlight."

He answered, "That's right. I am in the process of repairing it. I had a crash in low cloud."

I asked, "I hope you weren't hurt."

He laughed, "Only my pride was hurt. I am coming to Nairobi tomorrow. I wondered if we could meet up."

I answered, "That would be marvellous. Would you like to stay. I have plenty of room."

He said, "That's really kind."

I replied, "Great, do come for supper. I live in the end house of three opposite the CAIS in Lower Kabete."

He replied, "I know just where you are. One of my jobs is to pick up some AI straws. That will be handy. See you for supper."

I answered, "I will look forward to it."

I put down the phone. Then I worried that I had been too forward. I hoped that I had not given him the wrong impression. One of my jobs in the morning would be to go into Westlands and buy some bedding for the spare room. I suddenly blushed. I was being ridiculous. He would not be expecting to share my bed!

I was nervous and over excited the following evening. Matua had taken the arrival of a man to stay as normal. He had happily made up the spare room. He had even put some wildflowers in a jug. I did not possess a vase.

Beaver barked which alerted me to Percy's arrival. He was a short man of about forty with a wide smile. He made me laugh, as where in the UK a man might bring a bottle of wine or some chocolates, Percy brought a crate of beer.

He was very enthusiastic about the microlight. He said that all his chums had laughed at him. Most of them had light aircraft. He said that microlights were much cheaper to run, and he had only needed to make a short airstrip on his farm. I wondered if Kabete club would let me land beside the golf course. Percy said that I would be able to land on the field in front of my house. I was very dubious as there were several groups of high blue-gum trees in the vicinity.

He was easy to get on with. He loved his beer and encouraged me to drink several pints. I was soon slightly tipsy. I was very relieved when Matua brought in the food. Then I had a real piece of luck. Percy said that his farm was not very large, so he supplemented his income by taking camel safaris. He had come to agreement with the Samburu elders at Archers Post. They kept his camels for him, and he paid them. He also employed men to lead the camels when he took a safari. Part of the attraction for the safari was that there were no motor vehicles involved.

He normally had ten guests. He had five riding camels, so the guests spent half their time riding and half the time walking. He said that all his guests seemed to be easy-going people which made it easy for him. He said he needed forty other camels to carry baggage and supplies. If his normal drinking was anything like that night, he would need several camels just to carry the beer!

He told me that he only went in the dry season and so he did not take tents. He did take beds and mattresses together with bedding. He only trekked in the hot country. It sounded quite an adventure. I wondered if I could organise something for my government safaris. I was sure Dick would buy some camels for me.

Percy claimed that his camels did not get sick. I rather doubted that and thought it was perhaps the beer talking. However, he said he would be happy for me to blood test them on a regular basis. As well as blood testing them I could examine their skins and do a count of the number of ticks which were present. I made a mental note to brush up on my tick identification.

Mercifully I had not had drunk too much beer and steered Percy to his room and me to mine without any problems. I did not go instantly to sleep and lay awake worrying that I was not attractive enough for Percy to make a pass at me. Did I really want him to try. I had another brilliant idea. I could set up a series of fly traps on his safari route. This would certainly count as work but would also possibly get me an invitation on a safari. With these thoughts I slept.

I was dreaming when Matua brought in my tea. I think that I was dreaming of fighting off Percy who morphed into a giant tsetse fly. Drinking my tea calmed me down. I had to be attentive and bright to remember all the information which I could glean from Percy about the microlight.

Percy decided to make his first call to see the microlight. He said he would come back after that to pick up his semen supply from CAIS, together with his supply of liquid nitrogen. Much of the AI on small farms was performed with fresh semen. This had to be delivered twice a week. Percy's farm might not be that large, but it was classified as a large farm and therefore used deep frozen semen.

I was not the only person who had some different agendas. I could see that a small airstrip at Lower Kabete would be very useful for Percy, once he had repaired his microlight, to collect his deep-frozen semen. I knew that the road from Nyeri was tarmac but travelling by microlight door to door would be much quicker and easier. Percy was very enthusiastic about me constructing the microlight. He said if he could do it, he was certain that I would be able to, particularly as I would have Stanley and Morton to help me. He gave me good advice which was to concentrate on putting the engine together first rather than the airframe, because the airframe would take up so much space in the hanger.

His other good piece of advice was to get two lots of overalls so one could be in the wash at any one time. His much more dubious advice was not to wear anything under the overalls, in the theory that you did not want ruin all your underclothes by getting oil over them. In reality I suspected he had dreams of watching me changing.

The manufacturers of the microlights were helpful as there were two large toolboxes on wheels to keep the special tools which they provided, in some semblance of order. I made sure that Stanley and Morton did not take any of the tools away to use on the Landrovers down in the transport yard.

After Percy had left, I got on my motorbike and went into the shops to get overalls which would fit me. I was not going to spend my time wearing overalls which were too big for me and would have a crutch hanging down to my knees. I did not get much choice of colour. I picked red which I thought looked sexy. I did take Percy's dubious advice and wore nothing under them. It was so lovely working in the warm temperature I felt a liberated girl.

Stanley, Morton, and I set too, after the morning coffee break. So, Dick found me in the mini hanger. He had a present for me. It was a double barrelled 4.10 shotgun pistol. He had found it in his gun cabinet. It belonged to the LMD and was meant to be used by him as personal protection, when he took the money out into the bush to pay for the cattle. He thought that it would be useful for me on safari to shoot birds for the pot. He no longer took it with him as the new government instructions for handling large amounts of cash had changed. He now would get a police escort. He said as I was a Kenyan civil servant, he could easily issue the gun and ammunition out to me after I had got a gun licence from the local police in Kabete. He did warn me that they would have to come out and visit my house to see where my gun cabinet was positioned.

I was delighted and got him to promise to let me pay when we next went to the smorgasbord at the New Stanley Hotel. However, I was so enjoying working on the engine that I did not stop for lunch at the Vet Lab canteen that day. I was then starving when I eventually got home.

Niels also helped me on the microlight from time to time, but he said, Elisabeth had made him promise never to go in the contraption. I thought that it was best if I did not tell anyone that my guide and mentor on the construction project had crashed landed his own microlight.

The weather was so glorious that I made the most of my leisure time running with Beaver, as I wanted and enjoyed the exercise. I had met two girls whose husbands worked as vets at Kabete. They also worked at Kabete but under what was called local terms. This meant that they did not get paid overseas leave. Of course, as they were dependents, they got their fares paid. They persuaded me to play hockey for Nairobi Club. I did not have to pay to join Nairobi club as I could use my membership of Nanyuki club to reciprocate.

I enjoyed playing the games and meeting up with other girls. It did not seem to matter that I would miss some training sessions and games when I was away on safari. They also told me that their husbands played rugby for a club called Nondescripts which was based at Parklands near Westlands where I did my shopping. Nondescripts played games all over the country and even travelled to Tanzania and Uganda. On occasions they had combined tours when the girls would come to play hockey and the men would play rugby. I remembered one of my problems in England had been that I had found it difficult to socialise, because I was on call so often. I knew that deep down I was looking for a man. I might claim that I was happy on my own and that men were just a waste of space. In fact, that was not the case.

When there was an away game scheduled to play against Mombasa I readily signed up. I had a crafty idea to combine work with pleasure. I would schedule a meeting with the PVO Coast, James Roberton on the Saturday morning. The North Eastern Province which contained at least half of Kenya's camels, came under James Roberton as it was felt that there was not enough work to justify a vet, let alone a provincial vet in the North Eastern Province.

Most of the hockey team and the rugby team were going to drive down. I knew that the road trip of over three hundred miles would be interesting as the middle third went through Tsavo National Park. As I could not realistically leave until 4.00 pm this part of the journey would be in the dark. I would only get a fleeting glimpse of the game. I therefore elected to go on the overnight train.

This left at 6.00 pm on Friday evening and arrived in Mombasa at 8.00 am on Saturday morning. There were four of the girls coming down on the train and eight of the boys. It was a happy group who met at the station. Stanley gave me a lift in.

We were booked into double compartments. They all were in the same carriage. I was sharing with a single girl called Susan. We knew that for the first small bit of the journey we would be going beside Nairobi National Park. Susan and I decided to remain in our compartment and do some game watching. The two other girls, Martha and Eve were brighter than us. They realised we were in the next-door compartment to them which had a communicating door. Soon they were knocking. It was good to open up because it seemed to give us more space.

The others had seen much more game on other trips than I had. I was fascinated with what I could see from just the train: Giraffe (which I was told were called Masai Giraffe), Common

Zebra (I had seen Grevey's Zebra near Isiolo), Wildebeest, Impala, Common Waterbuck, Eland, Coke's Hartebeest and Wart Hoggs.

We left the Game Park and went through a town called Athi River without stopping as dark was falling rapidly. We all then walked down the train to get to the buffet car. We split up so Susan and I were sitting with two Rugby players, Rick, and Jeff. They were nice enough lads but a little young for us, however we chatted away. They were both at University in South Africa. They had been born in Kenya and so spent their vacations here. I imagined that they were good players as they seemed big and tough.

The food was amazing considering that it had all been cooked on the train. There was leek and potato soup with a warm bread roll. This was followed by a small fillet of tilapia (a freshwater fish caught in Lake Naivasha). Then there was cottage pie and cabbage. Finally, there was jam roly-poly pudding with custard before a cup of coffee. The whole lot was washed down with a couple of beers.

When we got back to our compartments, they had been made into two bunk beds with crisp white sheets and pillowcases. There was a small basin to wash our hands and faces. There was a loo at each end of the carriage.

The rhythm of the train soon sent me to sleep. I was the first to wake. I quietly let the blind up so that I could see the quick dawn rise. We were in Tsavo National Park. I saw two herds of elephants; one was crossing a large hump of rock. There was no delay. The leading animal obviously remembered the best path and confidently navigated the easiest path across the smooth rock. It was wonderful that the train was going so slowly. I did some mental arithmetic. The journey of 310 miles was taking us 13 hours. We were only averaging 23 miles an hour.

I was reluctant to stop viewing, but I had to go to the loo. I scared the pants off one of the boys when I came out. He nearly lost his towel. I suppose my nighty was rather revelling. Susan had woken up by the time I returned, so we both went along to the dining car for breakfast. None of the rest were up so we sat on a table for two. We could still look out and watch the game.

The breakfast was a full English which included porridge. However, they managed to fry the eggs without breaking the yolks I never found out. It was very tasty. By the time we got back to our carriage the beds had been stripped and the bunk had been pushed up so that the carriage was in seating mode. We had left the park, but the land was still dry with thick bush. I remembered the map showing the distribution of tsetse flies. I was sure I remembered that they were still found outside of the park. It would be very difficult to keep cattle in this area. I saw a station called Mackinnon Road which I remembered was fifty miles from Mombasa. The air was getting much hotter. We had lost four thousand and five hundred feet.

Suddenly the land got greener. We had reached the coastal belt. We passed a station called Mariakani and the railway started to twist more as we came down the final thousand feet. Then I saw the sea. The Indian Ocean was a beautiful blue. We crossed a causeway and came into a very hot Mombasa. There were several of the opposition there to meet us. We introduced ourselves. Then I left them to lookout for the veterinary driver. I could recognise him by his khaki uniform. His name was Karissa which I thought was slightly strange as I had a girlfriend in England called Karissa. This Karissa was certainly very masculine with a wide smile. I managed to greet him in Swahili. He took me to a GK Landrover, and we drove off Mombasa Island along the causeway beside the railway track. There was a dreadful smell which I gathered was a combination of the public tip, the abattoir, the town dairies, and the veterinary office.

Karissa had told me that they started work at 8.00 am. It was now 8.30 am so there was quite a bit of activity. I was very hot in my dress. Susan had kindly taken my hockey kit and overnight things.

I had lost Karissa and I was now led by the messenger called Jacob down a long line of offices. The end one was signed, 'Personal Assistant to the PVO Coast Province'. I suddenly had a fit of nerves as Jacob opened the door for me. I was hit by a blast of cold air from the air-conditioning. It made me shiver and my nipples hardened. I hoped they would not show through my flimsy bra and light cotton dress. I read the sign on the desk. The PA was called Silas. He was very friendly, and we shook hands. He said he hoped I had had a good train journey. He knocked on the inner door. A very irate voice shouted, "Enter."

With a lot of trepidation, I went in. The PVO did not get up, nor did he make any attempt to find me a chair. He looked at me with a frown on his face in a similar way to the surgery professor at vet school had, when I had been caught not attending an afternoon's practical in the post-mortem room.

Then he said, "I don't like being used as an excuse for a jolly down to the coast."

I did not reply. Nor did I hang my head. I looked at a point three inches above his head without flinching.

He said, "Silas should not have had you picked up from the station. It is against regulations for non-government employees to ride in GK vehicles."

I now was very angry, "I am a Kenyan Veterinary Officer. I am only paying you a curtsey visit as I will be working in The North Eastern Province which I understand comes under your control. I have read your last two annual reports. There was no mention of you visiting the area in either of them. I won't take up any more of your time. I will copy you in on my reports. Goodbye."

I had lit the blue touch paper, "How dare you?"

He got up knocking his chair over backwards and came around his desk. He was a short rotund man, may be four inches taller than me. I thought he was going to hit me. He was very red in the face even in the freezing cold air-conditioned room. He was wearing a white shirt, white shorts, and knee-length white socks. He was a classic misogynistic colonial.

At that moment the door swung open to reveal another short man dressed in khaki who said, "Your PA informs me that you are the only two vets within three hundred miles. Which one of you is going to replace the uterus of my mare?"

I replied, "I am Tanya Fox. I will replace the uterus for you. I am extremely proficient at that task."

I had never seen a prolapsed uterus in a mare. I had seen several in cows. I assumed mares were similar. I glanced at the PVO. He looked very relieved. He obviously did not want to get his 'whites' dirty. "Report back to me Miss Fox when you have finished."

I had been dismissed. I followed the man who introduced himself as Chris Patten out of the office.

He said, "She is in my horse trailer with the foal in front of her. I suggest you leave her on board as she was a bugger to load. My syce will hold her head."

I replied, "Certainly, the trailer will be like a set of stocks. I will want you to hold her tail. Has she cleansed?"

He answered, "Yes, I checked, the whole lot was there."

I replied, "That's a relief."

We had been joined by Jacob who I asked to get a bucket of water and a tablet of soap. I got Chris to lower the back ramp but to leave the bar in place The groom was already at her head. Chris looked surprised when I took off my dress, saying, "I don't want to ruin my dress. I am only down here to play hockey."

Chris laughed, "I had heard that James Roberton, the PVO did not like to get his hands dirty. You had better take your bra off. It's white and will get very bloody. All the local Giriama women walk around topless."

I did as he suggested, thinking, what would my mother say. Mercifully she was many thousands of miles away.

I talked to the mare as I cleaned up her perineum, with Chris holding her tail. Then after I had thoroughly washed my hands and arms, I started to push the organ back into the animal. It was a daunting task. Slowly I made headway until I just needed one more push, but I did not dare to move my hands as I was sure the organ would come out again. I leant forward and used my head. With blood and mucous dripping down my face, I felt the uterus go back through the vulva. I used one arm to make sure that it was in the correct position.

Chris looked at me, "You look a right mess, but well done. I never thought that you would do it." As I came down the ramp, I realised the PVO was standing aghast looking at me."

He said, "Next time that you come to my province. I suggest you are appropriately dressed."

He turned on his heel and went back to his office. Jacob brought me another clean bucket of water. I washed my hair and my upper body. He then gave me a towel to dry myself.

Chris had closed the ramp. I suggested, "I would inject her with penicillin for three days so that the womb does not become infected. She should be able to breed again. There is no reason for the womb to come out a second time."

He nodded his head. "My farm is eight miles up the road towards Nairobi. You are very welcome to stay if you come down again."

I asked, "How do you manage to keep your horses alive as you must have some tsetse."

He answered, "I do a large amount of bush clearing within my wide fire breaks. I also spray any vehicles entering with insecticide. I try to keep the tsetse out."

I catalogued this information in my brain in case I ever needed to bring camels to the coast. I put my dress on and asked Karissa to give me a lift into Mombasa Sports Club where I knew the rest of the team would be meeting. I never let on to my teammates what I had been up to.

We were helped by coming from five thousand feet. It felt as if we had wings on our heels. Both teams won. The cold showers were very welcome. Susan had warned me to get rehydrated with non-alcoholic drinks after the game. Apparently, you got absolutely plotto if you had even just a couple of beers straight after a long violent exercise. What most people drank was a very refreshing lemonade with freshly squeezed lime juice.

There was then a most enjoyable Bar-B-Q at the club followed by a dance. I was introduced to a couple called Angela and Alan Barret who were my hosts for accommodation. They were a friendly couple with two teenage boys. I was glad that I did not have to strip off and treat a mare in front of the boys as they seemed mesmerised by my body. I tried to get them to dance but they were too shy. In the back of the car on the way to their house in Nyali they kept away from me as if I had leprosy.

They had a beautiful house on the beach. I was shown to my room which had a glass door which led on to a patio overlooking the beach. It was so beautiful. I sat on my bed enjoying the romantic view. Then I was very naughty. I turned out the lights in my room and took off my clothes. I quietly opened the door and went across the patio. I ran across the beach and dived into the breakers. It was so exciting. I then made my way back to the house. Just on the edge of the patio was a shower. The water was fresh and felt very cold. It was so lovely and refreshing. The air was so hot that I was nearly dry by the time I reached my room. I made sure that I was completely dry before slipping under the single sheet.

The sun woke me in the morning. I put on my bikini and very demurely went for a swim. I could not believe how wonderful it was having the whole beach to myself. I came back and washed my feet in a plastic bowl on the patio. I then went and had a warm proper shower and shampooed my hair. I was rinsing myself off when a movement outside the window caught my eye. I was being watched by the two boys.

I was at a loss to know what to do. I decided, probably wrongly, to totally ignore them. I had no experience of the behaviour of young teenage boys. I finished rinsing myself then I dried my body, before wrapping a towel around me. I then put my hair in a towel to dry so that it would be easier to combe out. I walked into my room and hastily put om my bikini before wrapping the towel back around me and going on to the patio where Angela was laying out the breakfast. There was a melon like fruit which she was cutting in half. I asked her what it was. She told me that it was a pawpaw or what others called a papaya. She said she was sure I would enjoy it with a squeeze of a fresh lime. She was right. Alan and the boys joined us. Nothing was said about the boys spying on me.

It was lovely having breakfast out in the sun in my bikini. My hair soon dried. Alan asked me if I knew how to sail. I told him I had sailed dinghies when I was a teenager, but I had never sailed anything bigger. He told me they were members of the dinghy sailing club on Mombasa Island. He asked if I wanted to go. I jumped at the chance. Angela said, "I'm delighted. I am not very good. The boys sail as a pair. I have to crew for Alan. He is very competitive and gets cross with me if I make a mistake. I will be happy reading the Sunday papers."

We set off back across Nyali Bridge to the sailing club. They sailed in the water between Likoni ferry and Port Reitz harbour. It was a little scary as all the big ships came into this harbour. In theory the rule on the water was that steam gave way to sail. This obviously was not a reality when you were considering a small two-person dinghy and an enormous ocean-going freighter. The freighters blew their foghorns and the dinghies just had to get out of the way.

They signed me in as a guest when we arrived. Then we had to walk into the bar to sign up for the racing. The boys were going to be sailing in a yacht called an Enterprise. This was fairly basic with two sails, a mainsail and a jib. The helm's man worked the tiller and the mainsail. The crew had to work the jib. There obviously had been arguments in the past. The eldest was the helm's man for the first race and the younger boy would take the helm for the second race.

Alan and I were going to be racing a much faster craft called a 505. Alan was very much in charge. I was just the crew. I knew where the boy's had got their habit of being voyeurs. Alan was the same. I had not noticed when we had had our breakfast and I was only wearing my bikini. Now as I stripped off my shorts, I knew he was watching me. I'm not shy but his scrutiny annoyed me. In some way this was a benefit. I decided to keep my shirt on to protect my shoulders from the sun. I had read that you could get burnt by the reflection of the sun off the water. We then had to put on a life vest. Alan insisted that he checked the front straps of mine to make sure they were tight enough. I pre-emptied him when I put on my harness on my bottom, "Alan, you have no need to check. I know precisely how big my bottom is!" The harness had a ring on the front. When we went about, I had to unclip this from a stay from high up on the mast, move over the boat underneath the boom and clip on again when we were on the other tack. I also had to move the jib across. I was going to be a busy girl.

We went out before the race to do some practicing. It actually was not that difficult. I just had to get the timing right. However, I could see how a husband and wife team could fall out. Perhaps I should have denied any knowledge of sailing and read the Sunday papers! After we had done several practices, I realised that my bottom which was barely covered by my skimpy bikini was right in Alan's face as I climbed under the boom. Perhaps I should have kept my shorts on.

I put my worries behind me and enjoyed the thrill of moving fast just above the water. My job was to lean out as far as I could and arch my back so that the leverage of my weight compensated for the wind in the large mainsail. I just had to trust Alan to control the tiller and the tightness of the mainsail-sheet to keep the boat on an even kneel. I learnt that the boat did not have a kneel but a movable centre plate which Alan had put down after we had left the beach.

I reflected on men's behaviour. Did girls encourage them by wearing very little. I suppose we do. The Victorians used to have beach huts which went into the sea so that the ladies who were fully clothed could maintain their modesty. Yet certainly I had not encouraged the boys to spy on me in the shower. Also why was it fine for the Giriama ladies to walk around topless and yet European and Moslem ladies could not. Different cultures were hard to understand. I had been entirely happy with the Boran men wandering about naked except for a blanket thrown over one shoulder, when we were in the NFD. I would have been taken aback if Dick had done the same.

Alan was certainly very competitive. I also wanted to win the race, but if something went wrong, I did not feel the need to get cross about it. The two different styles of dinghy had different handicaps, called a harbour rating. Because our boat was much faster than the boat that the boys were in, we had to, not only beat them, but also beat them by a considerable time margin. Alan, not only had to out sail the other 505s, but also, he had to get a bigger enough lead to beat the enterprises. As it was in both the races, the better enterprise crews won overall. Alan was pleased that we were the second 505 overall.

I wanted to pay for the family's lunch in the sailing club to thank them for my stay. I was not allowed to as no cash was used; everything was paid for by the members signing a bar chit. I ended up insisting that they came to stay in my house when they came up to Nairobi.

In the afternoon I had another excitement. We went across the island to the water-ski club, which was on a much quieter piece of water, Tudor Creek. This was around from Nyali Bridge. We had to go down a long flight of stone steps to get to the water's edge. There was only a small beach with folk sunbathing. What was more important was the bar and the jetty. Once again it was a club so that I had to be signed in as a guest. It was more relaxed than the sailing club, perhaps because of the younger age of the members. There were several boys and girls of similar ages to Alan and Angela's boys. The barman was a cheery coastal man call Sealion. He looked after and drove the club's speed boat. There were three other privately owned boats. Soon the boys got turns water skiing. I went with Angela in the boat. Alan drove. The boys were both very accomplished. The eldest could start on one ski standing on one ski in the shallow water. The younger boy told me that he had not mastered that yet, but he started on one ski in deeper water.

Angela drove when Alan had a ski. There was no doubt that he was very good on one ski. Angela drove him very fast. Twice she took him through the slalom course. Each time that he turned sharply around a buoy he seemed to almost stop the boat. I was pleased that Angela had a ski. She had a very good figure for a girl who had teenage sons. She might not have gone so fast, but she was very graceful and went through the slalom course. Then it was my turn. Angela had briefed me on what to do when the others had been skiing. For a start she made me wear a lifejacket mainly because she said my bikini top would probably come off if I didn't. She also made we wear my shorts. She said I could easily wash then off in fresh water, and they would dry very quickly in the sun. She whispered to me, "Your shorts will protect you from getting a douche and an enema when you are learning. What you need to do is have your two skis about three feet apart, then it is easier to balance. Lean back with your arms straight and keep your knees bent. Your bottom will be dragged through the water. You must keep your knees bent until you feel you have got your balance and only then can you slowly straighten your legs. All the time you must keep your arms straight. Don't look so worried. You will be fine."

I was nervous. Angela came in the water with me to help me to get my skis on. Then she stood in the water which came above her waist and held me from behind. This steadied me. Alan and the boys were in the boat with the engine idling about ten yards away. Alan threw the handle on the ski-rope to me. I managed to catch it OK. Then he engaged the engine and drew away. The rope became taught, and I was pulled along. Then he hit the accelerator and I was off. I did just as I had been told. I felt the rush of water between my legs. Thank goodness I had my shorts on. I felt very open. I soon stopped wobbling and slowly straightened my legs. I was up. I kept my arms extended. It was now very exciting. I saw Alan put out his arm to indicate he was turning to the left. I had to put a little more weight on my left leg to follow the wake around. I still stayed in the calm of the wake as Alan accelerated the boat up the creek. Then I had to turn again. This time I went over the wake. There was quite a bump and I wobbled but mercifully did not fall. I seemed to be almost flying as I was on the outside of the circle as he turned for home. I leant inwards to cross the wake, hit a small wave and I fell. My instinct was to hold on to the rope. I was pulled through the water at great speed. I lost both skis. I certainly would have lost both bits of my bikini if I had not been wearing a lifejacket and my shorts. I could hold on no more and I let go. I soon bobbed to the surface.

The boat seemed miles away. I started to worry about sharks. They had been to collect my skis. Eventually they returned. I knew what was expected. I had to have another go. It was like falling off a horse. Getting my skis on was a real mission. Then I had to get in the right position with my knees bent to start again. There was no Angela to steady me. Alan threw the rope to me and slowly it tightened it up. He hit the throttle and I did everything wrong. I straightened my legs and pulled in with my arms. I fell headfirst into the water. This time I let go of the rope immediately and did not lose my skis.

Alan circled behind me. As he threw me the rope he shouted, "Keep your arms straight!" I was too waterlogged to shout back. I tried again. This time I kept my legs bent, felt the rush of water between my legs and kept my arms straight. I was determined to stand up and I did. I was totally knackered when I threw the rope away when I was near to the beach. Angela ran down to greet me and threw her arms around me, "I watched you through binoculars. You were doing well. You certainly hit the water very hard and then you great clot you held on to the rope. I thought for one dreadful moment that you had drowned."

I was too knackered really to say anything, but I knew that I would have another go when I came back down to the coast. I enjoyed my cup of tea out in the sun after I had washed off the salt water with a hose. My clothes were soon dry. It seemed too soon for us to start climbing the steps, but I am glad we had got going as I was only just in time for the train. The whole family came on to the platform to see me off. Susan wanted to know what I had been up to. She and several of the other girls had been to the south coast and spent the day on the beach. They also had nearly missed the train as there was a queue to get on the Likoni ferry.

Chapter 6

Sadly, the fast dusk came before we reached Tsavo Game Park, but we had a good supper and then I had a wonderful sleep. I was totally exhausted after all the sport and the dancing. Susan and I slept in so breakfast was a bit of a rush. Niels kindly met me at the station and so I was not late for work. Soon I was in my red overalls with Morten and Stanley putting together the engine of the microlight. In fact, because the instructions were very detailed the task was not that difficult and we made good progress.

Unfortunately, I could not keep the project under wraps. The word swiftly went around the Kabete boma. I got plenty of visitors to the hanger. Most were very helpful. I was glad that I had bought two sets of red, girls overalls as many of the visitors were female. The work on the engine went quickly forward. In a few days we had it secured with clamps to the work bench to make it firm. It was the size of an engine for a large lawn mower. To start it I had to pull a handle on a cord. It seemed quite an achievement when it fired into life. Assembling the airframe took much longer as all the nuts had locking pins.

While this was going on, the Vet Lab's farm manager, a delightful man, called Barnabas Toya had got his staff to flatten an airstrip on the paddock in front of my house. FAO also paid for the construction of a hanger.

Percy paid us an unexpected visit. I got him to look at the airstrip. He paced it out and said it was easily long enough even with the tall blue-gum trees on the far end. He was interested in the airframe. He was having difficulty getting parts to repair his from the USA. He drove off after stressing that if I had any problems, I was to contact him and he would be happy to come down to help.

Barnabas was obviously worried about me. He kindly got a wood cutting gang to fell a corridor of blue gum trees so that there was a gap for me to pass through the trees if I needed to in the microlight. I did not feel guilty as the blue gum trees were not native to Kenya and had originally been brought in from Australia. The gang made them into logs so Kabete residents had a useful store of wood for the colder months of the year mainly May and June and October.

At last, the airframe including the mounting for the camera was completed. It was time for me to man up and take off. There was a flying manual included in the crate with the airframe which I had read several times. Having put the plane together I knew exactly what the controls were. They were in fact very simple. There was a hand brake and a control column which turned the rudder on the small tail plane. There was a throttle which controlled the revs of the propeller. There were no gears. The lift was supplied by a large, four bladed helicopter like propeller at the back. To take off you pushed the throttle forward. The increased revs moved the microlight forward and turned the big propellor which lifted the microlight into the air. Although I described it as a microlight, it did in fact have some attributes of gyrocopter. To land you throttled back and the craft lost high and sank to the ground.

I had got Stanley and Morton plus two other Kabete drivers to help me to push the microlight out of the hanger and down the road to the field. Then wearing my motorbike helmet, facing into the wind, holding on the brake I increased the revs to their maximum, the microlight shot forward and I soon rose dramatically into the air. It was wonderful seeing the area from three hundred feet. I did a gentle turn and lined back up on the same course in front of the airstrip cutting the revs and settled gently down again. It was almost an anti-climax, but I could see

Stanley and Morton clapping. The manual claimed that the top speed in still air was forty-five miles an hour. I could carry enough petrol in the tank for three hours, so I had a range one hundred and thirty-five miles, enough to get me to Mweiga which was the nearest airstrip to Nyeri. I then could get to Isiolo on the next flight. When I got more experienced, I found I could get as far as Nanyuki from Kabete. I also found that I could take fuel in square aviation cans, strapped behind me. This could radically increase my range. I thought that it was sensible to purchase a small, short-wave radio so that I could communicate with the office in Kabete. I bought a second radio which we fitted into the Landrover. I then could talk to Stanley. I would need him to follow me by road when I started photographing the area so that we could count the camels in the NFD. I had several training flights around Kabete. I found that I could carry more weight. At this altitude I could carry a light person. Chatting to Percy I thought that at sea level I would be able to carry a normal sized man. He would have to sit behind me like a pillion passenger on my motorbike.

There was a considerable amount of mathematics required. I would need to keep taking photographs so that I could lay them all out, linking them together so that I could count the camels. It was going to be a long laborious process. Thank goodness the weather was dry in the NFD. Niels was so relieved that I was getting on with the job on the ground. He was happy to remain in Kabete and wait for the bundles of photographs to arrive. I would make a camp on an airstrip. We did not waste time and fuel flying back all the time. Because Stanley and Morton got a decent amount of money for subsistence allowance living out in the NFD, they were happy to remain with the microlight. I used to come home on the motorbike to play hockey on Saturdays, bringing the photographs which we had taken in the six days. Soon as we got further away from Kabete, I stayed away for three weeks at a time so that I had to forgo my hockey. I did keep myself fit running around the various airstrips. During the time I was up in the NFD, I joined Dick White on a buying safari in North Eastern Province. He bought over six thousand cattle in Wajir and then we went a further one hundred and ten miles north to El Wak which was on the border with Somalia. I was very careful not to fly the microlight into Somali airspace as they had a reputation of firing on any aircraft. By now I was confident about flying that distance without refuelling There was a very picturesque Arab fort overlooking the town. No one including Dick had any idea why it had been built. Dick bought another three thousand cattle in El Wak. We were both certain that they originated in Somalia. Finally, we flew up to Mandera which is, not only on the border with Somalia, but also with Ethiopia. I knew that at some stage Niels, and I would have to meet up with the vets in Ethiopia and Somalia to find out their numbers of camels and what diseases affected them. I did not think we would get much information out of Somalia, but I was more optimistic about Ethiopia as they were meant to have a good veterinary school and laboratory at Debre Zeit which was a few miles south of the capital Addis Ababa.

Dick bought another five thousand cattle in Mandera. I found it interesting that in all these remote outposts the veterinary staff seemed pleased to see us. It encouraged them that someone from Kabete was interested in them. I gathered that the PVO had never visited them, and he had been in post for nearly eight years.

It took us eight months to count all the camels in Kenya, living to the east of Lake Rudolf. There were camels to the west of Lake Rudolf, but FAO had decided to concentrate on those to the east. While we were carrying out our census, I spent days blood testing Percy's trekking camels at monthly intervals. I also with the help of the local veterinary scouts and the camel herders counted the ticks on the camels as best we could. Identifying the mature ticks was straight forward but identifying the immature ticks was more problematic. The species had different life cycles.

Some were just single host species and spent their whole lives on a single camel. Others might have two or three hosts as they matured. These were so called two host or three host ticks. Camels were not the only hosts. Several of the species would live on cattle, sheep or goats. Other species were said to suck blood from game animals. Various hunters had recorded these.

There were three important tick borne diseases which infected cattle, East Coast Fever, Anaplasmosis and Babesiosis. Luckily the ticks which spread these diseases did not occur in the NFD except on rare occasions. Cattle, sheep, goats and camels were not dipped in the NFD to kill the ticks. The animals and the ticks seemed to be in a natural balance.

I spent time with Horatio Little. He was friendly guy in his mid-forties. I think he was gay but, I was not totally sure. He was an extremely knowledgeable zoologist and he taught me a large amount, particularly about Trypanosomes. We worked closed together sharing a microscope. He never made a hit on me so either he was gay or just did not fancy me. I think he just enjoyed my company. I soon got expert at recognising *T. brucei, T. vivax and T. congolense*. These species caused disease in cattle, sheep and goats as well as camels. They could only be transmitted by tsetse flies. We both were very excited when we found our first *T. Evansii*. This was the only Trypanosoma which was exclusively found in camels and was spread by biting flies. We found it in a single camel belonging to Percy Gibbon when I had routinely tested them. A month later we found it in the same camel and Percy reported that this camel had lost weight. I flew up to examine the animal.

I now knew a little more about camels. This animal called Gnatty was definitely ill. With some reluctance I injected it with an anti-protozoal drug called Diminazene aceturate. I had read that the best place to find these trypanosomes was to look in the blood taken as a small drop from the ear and not to spread out the drop but to dry it and then stain it with a stain called Geimsa.

All the slides I had taken before had been from the tip of the camels tail and had been made into a smear. Apparently, the stain was named after a German zoologist, called Gustav Geimsa who had used it to stain and see malarial parasites.

Percy had brought Gnatty, and a friend called Delila back to his farm near Nyeri, so that he could nurse the sick camel. I got him to ring me with an update on her condition. I was delighted to hear that she had made a marked improvement in 48 hours. I had not been optimistic as I had found when I got back to the lab at Kabete that the sample was full of parasites. Percy sent down another sample from Gnatty in a week and I could only find a single parasite. However, to be on the safe side I sent up a single injection to treat Gnatty a second time. This seemed to clear the parasites from Gnatty who made a total recovery.

Percy wanted me to let him have sachets of the Diminazene aceturate which were to be dissolved in boiling water and then the liquid had to be injected subcutaneously. I went to see Terry Stokes, the DVS. He agreed with me that it would be wise to keep this drug in veterinary hands and so with the backing of the DVS, who was the God of the veterinary world in Kenya, I had to tell Percy that I was not allowed to give him any Diminazene. I expected that there would be fireworks, but surprisingly he was very pragmatic. I think Percy was grateful that he was getting all this free veterinary work which was being paid for by FAO.

Gnatty and Delila went back to Isiolo. I continued to take blood samples from all of his camels. I made sure that the blood was taken from the ear and that it was examined as a so-called thick smear.

I was summoned one morning to see the DVS. I thought that I was in for a telling off like I used to get from the three partners in the practice in Chippenham. This was not the case. Neils was already in his office, as was Michael, John and Charles. The DVS said how pleased he was with the completion of the camel census. He then told us the bad news which was that there was a deterioration in the political situation between Kenya and Somalia and that there was to be no visits to that country. However, Dick White was going to continue to buy cattle in Kenya regardless as to whether they were locally bred cattle or from either of our neighbours. What was more important for Neils and me was that he was going to start to buy camels. These were destined to go by boat to the Middle East. After the meeting broke up, the DVS took me to one side, "Tanya, I want you to charm James Roberton, the PVO for The Coast and The North Eastern Provinces, as the camels will originate from The North Eastern Province and have to travel through The Coast Province. I had rather mixed messages from the PVO coast when you went down to Mombasa. Initially he seemed very hostile but latter he seemed to view your visit more favourably. Perhaps I could hear your side of the altercation."

I did not want to tell tales and in fact I did see The PVO's point of view. I replied, "I think he was cross because he thought he was being used as an excuse for me to visit the coast which in some ways was true as I did play hockey."

Terry asked, "I'm intrigued as to why his attitude to you softened?"

I could not resist answering, "I think he was impressed by my naked chest."

Terry chuckled, "Did you take him with you to the beach sunbathing?"

I replied, "No I did not want to get my clothes all bloody as I had to replace a prolapsed uterus in a mare at the veterinary office."

Terry laughed heartily, "I think I must come with you to do more clinical work in future."

I answered, "I know I should be cross with you for making such a sexist remark, but actually I am not that bothered. It seems very racist to me that African ladies at the coast bare their breasts, but it is taboo for European ladies to do the same."

He smiled, "I will have to discuss that fact with my wife and my two grown-up daughters. They are all at home would you like to come to supper tonight?"

I replied, "I would like that. I will be very demure with my attire!"

I left him laughing. The evening was good fun. His daughters took my side of the argument, his wife vehemently took a very Victorian stance. I hoped I had not caused too much of a family rift.

When I saw the DVS three days later in the coffee room, He whispered to me, "When you were in my office the other day, we were so busy discussing your attire that I forgot to ask you. I want you to go to Machakos to go and see The PVO Eastern as Marsabit, Meru and Kitui Districts are in his province. You have been counting camels, but I think it would be good for you to touch base with the PVO. His name is Tim Stockman."

I asked, "Is he fierce?"

He replied, "No I think you will like him. He plays hockey and rugby."

The DVS said no more, and I thought no more about it, except that I decided on my next trip up to the NFD to go to the East of Mount Kenya and spend a night in Meru Game Park which I had been told was very remote and exciting.

I had an enjoyable day on Saturday playing hockey in the afternoon followed by a party in the evening at Parklands. I was due to blood test some camels at Mado Gashi on the Monday morning, so I thought it was quite reasonable to spend the night at the self-service lodge in Meru Game Park on the way. I set off in the microlight on Sunday morning with some provisions, having asked Stanley and Morton to meet me at Mado Gashi on Monday morning. Stanley said they would arrive on Sunday night, I suspected so that they could claim the generous living out allowance, as Mado Gashi was said to be in a dangerous area. I arrived at the small lodge at lunch time to find a very distraught lady who I recognised. The European population in Kenya is very small and so it was very normal to bump into people one knew. However, this was unusual because this lady was Mrs. Cunningham who I had had lunch with many months ago in Wiltshire. They were out on a family holiday. She was worried because her husband had set off at dawn with their six daughters to go on a game run. They were due back for breakfast. I could understand why she was worried. I volunteered to go out and look for them. Mrs. Cunningham who insisted that I called Jill, was slight in stature but was, as I knew from her husband, very forceful. I did not try to dissuade her from coming with me. I had no concerns with the weight as we were only at 1500 ft.

Meru is a large park. We had little to go on except her husband called Charles had said to her that they hoped to reach the Tana River. We headed southeast following the road. It was spectacular game viewing. In twenty minutes, we could see the Tana River. There was the Landrover in the middle of the river. As we approached there was some expansive waving from the figures on the southern bank. However, the road was much straighter on the northern bank, so I decided to land there. Historically I would have been terrified, but now I was quite an experienced pilot and I landed without any difficulty. Jill and I then walked the 100 yards around two corners to the river. We brought some of my food. Then Jill bravely came with me, wading through the river across the causeway. The water came to the middle of our thighs. As you can imagine there was an excited family reunion. The girls set upon the food like locusts.

Apparently, the eldest daughter called Sally had been driving. Unfortunately, she had managed to come off the causeway with one front wheel, when the vehicle was ten yards from the further bank. Water had come like a wave over the bonnet. The plugs had got wet, and the engine had died. Charles put his arm around my shoulders and said, "What's the plan, Tanya?" I had liked

Charles when I first met him. That question made me like him much more.

I replied, "I could fly back to the lodge and get help, but being Sunday afternoon that will be difficult and will take considerable time. I think I can manage to get the Landrover out to this near bank. Then we will let it dry out. Then we can turn it around and if you stay on the causeway, you can come across to drive back to the lodge."

Sally butted in, "I'm so sorry Mummy to cause you all this worry." Jill showed her metal, "Think no more about it dear. I have had the most marvellous game flight."

Now I had to get the Landrover on to dry land. "We will all push, if you drive Charles. What I want you to do is to use the battery to get us back on to the cause way. When we are all ready, I will give a shout. You will turn on the ignition, with the Landover in first gear, low range, you will press the starter and the vehicle hopefully will lurch forward on to the causeway. Save the battery. We will push it along, after that."

That is what we did. With a herculean effort we got the front wheels out on the bank out of the water. Then we opened the bonnet and dried the inside of the distributor. The hot Kenyan sun dried out the plugs and the rest of the electrics. Twenty minutes later Charles started the engine which, after an initial splutter, was soon running on all four cylinders. Then with me walking in the middle of the causeway he drove the vehicle back to the northern side of The Tana and back to the microlight.

To try to cheer her up I asked Sally if she would like to come with me in the microlight back to the lodge. She jumped at the chance. We saw a lot of game and had a good late lunch at the lodge on a big table in front of the six double bandas. The Cunninghams occupied four of them. I had the fifth banda and the sixth was empty. In the afternoon I took the five younger girls up for short game flights. Charles insisted he had a flight as well. I was glad my fuel tank was only a quarter full as he was quite heavy. Actually, I had no problems taking off as the airstrip was over 1200 yards.

They were a lovely family, and it was a most enjoyable evening. So much so that I persuaded them to all come and stay with me at Kabete before they flew home. The four youngest girls put up camp beds and made my living room into a dormitory. Matua coped wonderfully with all the visitors.

We were now getting a picture of possible diseases which might infect camels. There was good news as the majority seemed to be very healthy and live long lives. What was not so good was that our tsetse fly traps were yielding larger numbers of flies than had been seen before. Horatio warned me that we would be likely to encounter both chronic and acute trypanosomiasis if camels strayed into these areas. Obviously, the locals were aware of this and they avoided these areas. I was determined to learn more Masai which was spoken not only by the Masai in Masailand but also more importantly by the Samburu and Rendile in the NFD who were in the same tribal group. It was very similar to the language spoken by the Kipsigis tribe. My Swahili by now was virtually fluent. Many of the older Samburu and Rendile spoke Swahili but not the young guys who did the cattle herding. There were hopes to get more education to the children and this would include English which was the official language of the country. Unlike in Tanzania where Swahili had been made the official language.

I spent some considerable amount of time studying the maps. The main problem that the LMD would have in getting camels which they had purchased in the NFD down to Mombasa would be crossing the Tana River where the riverine bush definitely harboured tsetse flies and the coastal strip which was likely to harbour the flies. I needed advice from the PVOs in Mombasa and Machakos as the DVS had advised. I was still wary of James Roberton, but I wanted to return to the coast. I would have to arrange a proper safari and NOT play hockey! However, I had no worries about Tim Stockman. In fact, if he was young enough to play rugby, I certainly wanted to meet him.

After an early breakfast I took off for the short journey of 40 miles to Machakos. I had already spoken to Tim's PA, Mohamidi Basu, who had suggested that I arrived when the office opened at 8.00 am on Monday morning. He obviously assumed that I was arriving in a Landrover. I decided really on a whim to fly in the microlight. I thought that I could easily walk from the airstrip into the veterinary office, if I could not find a suitable place to land any nearer. As it was, I landed at the club on the polo pitch. I checked into reception. The manger was a charming man. He was very welcoming and insisted that I had a cup of coffee with him. He told me that Machakos Club reciprocated with Nanyuki Sports. He said I was welcome at any time. He offered to drive me the veterinary office. I said I was happy to walk as it was only 500 yards.

Mohamidi Basu was a very tall polite Somali man. We got on well immediately, as he was most impressed that I had been to El Wak. He had been born there. He was very proud that he been born in the hospital. He smiled when he said that therefore he had been born on the right side of the border. He was also proud to be a Kenyan. He obviously knew the area well and was very knowledgeable about camels. I thought that he would be a very good contact. As there was no sign of the PVO we looked at the large map on the wall of his office together and discussed various routes that we could use to move camels. We were interrupted by a very rude farmer who barged his way into the office demanding to see the PVO.

Apparently, the District Veterinary Officer (DVO) was not in his office. The farmer called Reginald Fairbrother required a routine movement permit for a lorry load of his cattle to move to the slaughterhouse in Athi River that morning. The PA explained that the PVO was also not in his office but that he would investigate and see if a permit could be obtained. He left me alone with Reginald who glowered at me, demanding, "Who are you?"

I held out my hand, "I'm Tanya Fox."

He continued in a very irate manner, "What are you doing here? Shouldn't you be at school!"

Normally I would have made a joke about such a comment, but as he was so rude, I just said, "I have an appointment with the PVO."

This evoked a response of, "Bloody boy, he has more time for young girls that us ranchers."

At that point I rather wished that I was at school, in fact anywhere but in this office. However, Reginald was just a bully and my father had always stressed to me that I might be small but that it was very important to stand up to bullies. I said nothing but maintained eye contact. At that moment Mohamidi returned to the office with the movement permit book. "I'm sorry Captain Fairbrother. The clerk had made out the permit waiting for the DVOs arrival so that he could sign it. Apparently, a bus has broken down blocking the Nairobi Road near to the main Mombasa Road which is why neither the PVO nor the DVO have arrived."

I thought Reginald was going to explode, "Bloody hell. I need that bloody permit signed and I need it now!"

I thought, 'Silly man, a permit is the least of his worries. The lorry with the cattle won't be able to get down the road either.' However, I said, "There is not a problem Mr. Basu. I am a Veterinary Officer. I can sign the permit and Captain Fairbrother can get on his way."

Mohamidi bowed his head with relief and handed me the movement permit book. As I signed it, I could not resist saying, "Perhaps it's a good thing that I didn't go to school this morning, Captain Fairbrother."

If looks could kill, I would have been definitely dead. Mohamidi and I breathed a sigh of relief when the captain left the office. I decided that I had had enough of Machakos and so after shaking Mohamidi by the hand I walked back to the club. I thought that was the end of it, but to my horror Captain Fairbrother was demanding a drink in the bar and the manager was politely informing him that the bar was not open. I waved to the manager, "Thank you for your help. I will fly back to Kabete. I hope you get your cattle to slaughter Captain Fairbrother." I skipped out of the bar in case the captain threw something at me.

Two days later I received a book sized parcel in our office. It had come from the PVO's office in Machakos via The Diagnostic Laboratory with some diagnostic samples. I was delighted. It was a dictionary, English to Somali and Somali to English. Inside was written, 'With grateful thanks from Mohamidi Basu'. I immediately scribbled off a note to him inviting him to lunch if he was ever in Kabete. He was good company and often came to see me. He helped me to learn Somali.

I still needed a route to get the camels out of the NFD. So that I followed due protocol I wrote asking James Roberton whether he would like to join me on safari down the Tana River to catch Tsetse flies. As I hoped, he answered that he was inundated with work, but he wished me every success and that he would be grateful for my report in due course.

I set off on Monday morning in the microlight having had a good weekend in Nairobi playing hockey. Stanley and Morton had been happy to set off in the Landrover on Sunday morning to go via Garissa to set up camp near Bura north of the Tana River which was opposite Galole the District HQ for Tana River District which was south of the river. My flight was uneventful until I got to Bura. There was no airstrip and the road looked very rough and overgrown. I managed to contact Stanley on the radio, and he said that they were camped at a water hole called Dido four miles northeast of Bura where there was a flat open sandy place which would be a fine place to land. I had climbed higher to get a better radio signal so I stayed at altitude and soon could see the water hole in the distance. I think Stanley had been worried about me and so there was a rather enthusiastic reunion.

Stanley had set up two tsetse fly traps. One at Dido and one down on the river. It was now mid-morning but there were no flies in the trap at Dido. We drove to the one on the river. We had already caught five flies. It was what we had anticipated. The dangerous area was the two-mile strip either side of the river where there was much more luxuriate bush. It was interesting as Tana River District which was in Coast Province included this strip north of the river. The boundary was an arbitrary line drawn by the colonial administration years ago. North of that line was Garissa District which was in North Eastern Province. Stanley and I had a good laugh because our camp was in Garissa District and he together with Morton were entitled to a higher living out allowance. I doubted if the administrators at Kabete would ever check-up where we actually camped. We were very much alone. The area seemed devoid of people. That night I found out why.

It was dark and we had just finished our supper and two Somali men armed with 303 rifles walked into our camp. They had obviously been watching us. I knew that I should have been terrified but in fact I was not. They seemed surprised that I could speak some of their language. They were even more surprised when I offered them some tea and biscuits. Morton took my lead and took two of the seats out of the Landrover to make him and Morton some seats so that we could offer our visitors chairs. These men were 'shifta' which was a term used by Kenyans to cover any thief or bandit in the area. They knew all about tsetse flies. This water hole was very important to them as they could water their cattle here. They knew if they took their cattle to the river that they would get sick. I judged that if we had brought any cattle here there would have been a fight. I told them that I was interested in camels. They told me camels would get sick if I took them to the river.

I had done my homework in Kabete. I knew forty miles away towards the coast was a government holding ground called Bodhei. There they had spent a considerable amount of money clearing the bush and spraying the area to kill the tsetse. The plan had been to bring LMD cattle down to the coast and ship them in a boat to slaughter in Mombasa. The funds had run out. The bush had grown up and the tsetse flies had returned. The scheme had never got off the ground. I was determined to resurrect it for my camels. I would have to get agreement from the Somali elders who controlled the area. I asked the men whether they would take me to see their elders. They were surprised at my request but said that they would take me. They said there was no road, and the journey took four hours. They suggested that it would be best to do at least half the journey in the dark.

Stanley was concerned for my safety. I reassured him that I would be fine. The two men were happy to sleep on their blankets on the sand and we went to bed, Stanley and Morton in the back of the Landrover and me on my camp bed in the tent. 4.00 am seemed to arrive too quickly. I set off with two water bottles and three honey sandwiches which I had made the night before. I did not take the 4.10 pistol but left it locked in the secure box in the Landrover. Stanley and Morton did not wake.

It was scary, but the temperature was just right. I brought a silk head scarf and a kanga, a standard colourful piece of cloth worn by Moslem coastal ladies. I walked in a bush shirt and my shorts. My compass was on a cord around my neck. Everything else was in my small rucksack which I was used to carrying.

The men were amazing how they could follow a track in the moonlight. I just followed behind the leader and his friend followed me. The pace was fast. I was glad I was fit from playing hockey. I wished I had longer legs. I had plenty of time for reflection. I wondered why I was not afraid. I had not really been afraid of Mr. Gaston. That incident felt decades ago. After two hours we came to a road and stopped for a drink. Both men had gourds. They both laughed and accepted my honey sandwiches. Then we set off and the swift dawn arrived. Slowly it warmed up. I was glad we had set off in the dark as soon it became seriously hot. Our pace did not slacken. I wondered how long I could keep it up. I remembered what Dick had told me about drinking cold water in the heat, how it was not ideal as it brought you out in a sweat. I did not touch my water bottles.

The bush had got thinner we were now in what was really a desert. I knew that I would soon have to ask for a rest. I was getting dehydrated; I did not need a wee. Then I saw the village in the distance. The children ran out to greet us. They were fascinated by my long hair and came up to touch it as I bent down and got my kanga and headscarf out of my rucksack. I hoped that I was now acceptably dressed for Moslem company.

I was brought in front of five elders who were sitting on chairs under an awning. A chair was brought out of a hut for me. Nothing was said. I tried my rather poor Somali to greet them and enquired after their health. This was obviously acceptable as they smiled and replied that they were in good health. They asked after my health. I replied that I also was in good health. Then there was some conversation about the hot sun and the lack of rain. I asked about their cattle and was told they were well but were thin. I asked about their camels. Apparently, they were also well and were not thin. Quite a crowd had gathered. The children were very respectful and did not come too close. I noticed a young good-looking man had come to stand beside the elder in the right-hand chair. The elder in the middle chair asked me in Somali. Would I like some tea. I said I would love some. Then he said that he was pleased that I spoke his language, but perhaps we could continue in English which might be easier for me. I said in English that it would be. A table was brought, and ladies brought the tea in a large pot. It was poured into cups. I was ready for African tea which I knew had all been boiled together. There was milk already added and it was hot, and very sweet. I enjoyed it and did not break out in a sweat. I realised then that the elders obvious understood English but were reluctant to speak it.

The good-looking man was an interrupter. His English was excellent. He said that they knew about me and knew that I journeyed with Bwana White and that when I was alone, I flew in a strange aircraft. I laughed with him and asked how his English was so good. He said that he had been an illegal immigrant in the UK and worked as a taxi driver. He had got sick of the cold wet weather and had returned to Somalia where he was very happy.

The most senior elder interrupted and wanted me to answer some questions which had been troubling them. I told them to go ahead and ask.

They asked, "Was I working for The Kenyan Government."

I replied, "No I worked for the United Nations.

There was some fast Somali which I did not understand, but the young man translated, "Now they understand the strange red number plate on my Landrover."

The elders asked my real job, "I first had to count the number of camels which lived in Kenya."

There was more rapid Somali. The man said, "Now they understand why I flew up and down. Now they wanted to know what I was here for?"

I said, "I am here to find a safe way to bring camels down to the coast so that they don't get sick, and the Kenyan Government can sell them to the very rich, Arab people up north where all the oil is."

There was a lot of nodding of heads. Now all was understood. The elders stood up. The young man asked me to come near and kneel. I tried not to show any apprehension and I did as I was asked. The senior elder put his right hand on my head in a sort of blessing. Then the young man said. "You have the blessing of the tribe. You are free to come and go in our land. You are free to buy camels and to use our water holes. This is the reward for your bravery in coming to our land."

It was obvious that the meeting was over. The young man said that the two men would guide me back to my camp. That was that. I had come a long way from Wiltshire!

Chapter 7

I was tired but elated when I arrived back at the water hole. Stanley and Morton seemed very relieved by my return. The two Somalis disappeared into the bush, after waving their arms in farewell. On the following morning Stanley and Morton set off to return to Kabete and I flew east to the coast to land on the uninhabited island of Manda. There was an airstrip. This was used by visitors to the thriving island of Lamu. I could safely leave the microlight and walk the 400 yards to a jetty where I would be taken across to Lamu town. I expected to get a small dugout; however I was met by a very smart blue and white boat. It was really a launch with a small canopy over the controls. It was manned by two khaki clad boatmen who saluted me, "Welcome Memsahib." I shook their hands saying, "Please call me Tanya. Are you here to collect me or some important dignitary?"

The older boatman replied, "I am Benjamin, and my crew is Saul, we are from the Veterinary Department. We were warned on the radio of your possible arrival and then we saw your plane. Mr. Suleiman the District Livestock Officer (DLO) sent us."

I responded, "Well I am very grateful. It would have been a long swim!"

Benjamin laughed, "We have heard that you love the water, but we are glad to keep you dry."

I also laughed, "Who have you been talking to?"

Benjamin answered, "Sealion. He is a friend of ours. He comes up to service our boat engines. He told us what a polite kind lady you were."

I thought this is a good spot. I hopped into the boat. We set off to Lamu Town and were soon at the jetty. Mr. Suleiman was a strong looking Asian man. He was waiting for me and had a broad grin on his face. "Welcome to Lamu. I am very grateful to you for our radios we do not feel nearly so isolated now that we have one here and another on the mainland, which is mobile, so we can use it in Mkowe on the mainland jetty and at the two holding grounds Burgoni and Bodhei."

I replied, "I'm glad they are helpful. Did you hear me talking to Stanley?"

"I did. It was purely by chance. The LMD network are normally on between 7.30 am and 8.00 am. You must listen in. We can always help you with fuel and other supplies. Come into the veterinary office and have a cup of tea. It is much cooler in there. We don't have a fan because there is no electricity on Lamu, but it is an old building with high ceilings and a good airflow."

He was right the office was a nice temperature. I met Abdi the clerk and Ali the messenger. I learnt that the other veterinary staff lived and worked out of Mkowe on the mainland. Mr. Suleiman was a mind of information. He had records of all the tsetse flies that had been found in his district together with the tick species which had been identified. He was very pessimistic about bringing camels through the coastal strip. He was certain that they would contract acute trypanosomiasis within a few days. I was sad because this would make my plans very difficult. I enjoyed my cup of tea.

I noticed a big outboard engine on a stand. I asked, "Which boat does that go on?"

He replied, "It is for a rubber blow-up boat, which we can take in a Landrover when it is collapsed or on the roof rack when it is full of air. We often have to use it for cattle crossing the Tana River. The engine over there is 35 horsepower. On the sea we can go at 25 mph. We need that power as the current in the middle of the Tana is strong if there has been heavy rain on

Mount Kenya. Sealion tells me you have learnt to water ski. You are only light I think it would pull you OK."

I smiled, "I will have to get some skis and a rope."

He chuckled, "We will have to make sure the PVO does not hear about it."

I agreed, "He gave me a real dressing down for coming down to Mombasa to play hockey."

Suleiman was more encouraging, "I think he has forgiven you as you did such a good job on replacing the womb in that horse."

I laughed, "I think it was probably because I was striped to the waist?"

He smiled, "I am such a devout Muslim that whiskey turns to water as it passes my lips. Allah would have clouded my eyes to protect your modesty."

I laughed, "I think you are an old rogue. Should I have worn a head covering and worn a kanga coming on to the island?"

He replied, "No that would not be necessary to just come here to the office but it would be better if you did if you want to hold a meeting. Why don't you let my wife make you a buibui?"

I asked, "What's a buibui?"

He answered, "Let us go to Petley's Hotel, where you can stay. You will see some of the ladies wearing them. They are a black light cotton flowing garment. Buibui means spider in Swahili, so it is rather derogatory. The lady's heads are covered but their faces are not covered. I am told that some naughty ladies do not wear anything under them." Then he chuckled, "I expect you will be like that as you dressed like a Giriama lady in Mombasa!"

I had to smile. He was a humorous guy. He took me to his house, and I met his wife who was a sweet girl. She measured me and promised to make the garment for me. She had a sewing machine which she powered with her foot. Then we went to Petley's Hotel. This rather dark, but cool establishment, was run by two gay men, called Peter and Darki. They were a complete comedy turn. They welcomed Mr. Suleiman and me in the bar. I ordered cold 'Tuskers' for the four of us. Darki showed me to a room. He suggested that I might be happier sleeping on the roof as this was much cooler. I certainly agreed so that is what I did. There was an awning but absolutely no privacy. However, it was not overlooked. I would not be seen unless I went to the edge. There was a camp bed, a chair and table on which was a China washing bowl and large jug containing water. Darki very proudly showed the upstairs long drop, so I did not have to leave the roof but just could squat over a hole. It might have been very primitive, but I loved it.

After a second beer and a bowl of fish curry and rice I retired to my roof top for a siesta. Mr. Suleiman said if I came to the veterinary office at 4.00 pm, we could go for a walk, and he would show me some of the island. He told me to wear my swimsuit under my clothes as we could have a swim. We walked north initially along a stone sea front in front of houses and offices. The town ended and we walked along a beach which was covered in rather smelly seaweed. We came to a small fishing village called Shella, before we rounded a point which might be called a sand bar. Then we came to the most beautiful beach that I had ever seen in fact ever could imagine. We had a swim and then continued on this wonderful beach. After about a mile we left the beach and turned inland through a massive grove of coconut palms amongst which cattle were grazing. Eventually we arrived at the back of Lamu town. We went through a maze of tiny dark streets before coming to a big square with a Portuguese fort which was now the police station and jail. Mr. Suleiman claimed that the jail was always empty and there were only two policemen who never had to do anything.

We went to his house again and to my delight his wife had made my buibui. It was a wonderfully cool garment. No one could see that you were naked. I found it very sexy as I could realise all the men's imaginations running wild. Because of my dark brown eyes which were nearly black and my now very tanned face, I could easily be a young Arab Muslim girl. That was until I went into the bar at Petley's Hotel and ordered a cold tusker from their paraffin refrigerators!

The fish curry was slightly different from lunchtime but was equally delicious particularly with the fiery lime pickle, the chopped bananas, the chopped tomatoes, and mango chutney. I washed it down with two more tuskers and slept on my roof top. I felt as if I had woken from a coma when I struggled to get up at dawn. I was certain that I had kept half of Lamu awake with my snoring and that I would have been totally oblivious to being ravished by a tall dark and handsome stranger. No one was about in the hotel but there was a note to say my breakfast was in the fridge, it was a hand of bananas and two mangoes in a paper bag. I scuttled out of the hotel in my buibui to the veterinary department jetty. There were Benjamin and Saul in their immaculate uniforms standing on the jetty. Saul ran to get Mr. Suleiman, my drinking partner from last night. Benjamin helped me aboard the veterinary launch and congratulated me on my attire. Saul and Mr. Suleiman were soon on the scene, and we set off on the fifteen-minute boat trip to the jetty at Mkowe. The fresh air and four bananas helped to revive me.

We were met at the jetty by Kasim, a senior veterinary scout and Mabrouk, the head Lamu driver in a truck type Landrover. It was grey with an aluminium cab and a canvas covered truck body. Mercifully the windows had been removed as the four of us got into the cab which had the standard issue, three seats. We were very cosy. Normally when I was in the middle seat in our Landrover at home on the farm I sat with my legs astride the gear stick. This morning I was forced sit astride the handbrake almost in Mabrouk's lap. He did not seem to mind! The body of the truck was full of maize which had come in by boat from Mombasa and was to feed the large number of herdsmen who were bringing down the LMD cattle which Dick White had bought up north.

It took us half an hour to reach Burgoni holding ground which was a hive of activity. 300 steers were being mouthed in two side by side 30-yard-long cattle races. The head of each animal was help by tall very black Turkana herdsman naked except for a blanket fastened across his shoulders. A veterinary scout would grasp a tongue, pull it out of the mouth, and examine it for Foot & Mouth Disease (FMD) lesions. There were three hundred to examine. The first mob of fifty, twenty-five from each race had been examined within ten minutes of our arrival. They set off towards Mkowe to be loaded on to the cattle boat Bonanza which should arrive at 2.00 pm. They were herded by just three men. This apparently was double the normal rate of three per hundred for the trekking of larger mobs.

The races were quickly being filled up again. We left to journey on to the next much bigger holding ground at Bodhei. On the way we were attacked by hundreds of tsetse flies. I was very glad that I was wearing my buibui. The flies were not attracted to the black colour. They were attracted, according to Mr. Suleiman to white ladies, particularly pregnant white ladies. The three men thought that it was extremely funny when I told them that I had slept so well last night on the roof of Petley's Inn after all the tuskers that I had drunk, that I did not know whether I was not now pregnant, but that I certainly had not been pregnant, before I went to bed.

It took us forty minutes to reach the holding ground HQ. Once again this was a seriously busy place, The Landrover was backed up to the door of a shed and two men started to unload the maize. We walked to two more races of cattle. These were being blood tested by a drop of blood being taken from the tip of the tail on to a slide. These were dried in the warm air and stained with Geimsa stain before being carefully put in wooden slide boxes to keep them separate. They would return with us to Lamu island where they would be examined by Abdi and Ali who were also microscopists. If more than 5% had any trypanosomes, then that whole mob would be treated with a trypanocidal drug called Berenil injected subcutaneous into the brisket. They could not then go for slaughter for three weeks.

There were over two thousand steers on the holding ground. They all had been mouthed and treated with Berenil on arrival and were blood tested every three weeks. It was a constant job. Bonanza, the cattle boat took three hundred head of cattle three times a week. I did not have to be a clever mathematician to realise that Dick bought a large number of cattle. I asked Mr. Suleiman what happened if FMD was found. He said that movement was stopped for six weeks. Cattle for the abattoir would have to be procured from other sources like Mackinnon Road which was fifty miles away or Voi which was a hundred miles away. They came down on the train. He said once they had to get cattle from upcountry which meant a journey of over four miles. I felt sorry for the cattle. I also wondered if cattle procurement was one of the causes of Mr. Roberton's bad temper.

On the journey back to Mkowe we discussed the possible route for my camels. One idea was for bush clearing around Bodhei and on the route to Burgoni. Mr. Suleiman said that he would set the traps for the tsetse flies further west to Ijara, but he thought that there were no flies there, provided the cattle did not come near to the Tana River. He said he would show me a tractor and trailer which was at Burgoni which was used to carry stores but could be adapted to carry camels so in the dry season we could use that to bring the camels down to Mombasa. He did not think the jetty at Mkowe was big enough to take a ship which could take camels all the way to the Persian Gulf. He did say that regularly when the monsoon changed in April Dhows set off north carrying mangrove poles for building in the Persian Gulf. He wondered if they would be prepared to take camels.

Mr. Suleiman was a man of action. He would have made an excellent marshal for Napoleon or a general for the allies in the second world war. He said I should get more tsetse fly information on the holding grounds at Karawa and Sabaki between the Tana River and Malindi. I could try to get funds to do more bush clearing. Tsetse flies needed bush to breed. He had heard that there was scheme up near Lake Victoria where they were releasing sterile male tsetse flies to cut down the numbers of the flies.

He also suggested that there might be a way to get the camels down through Kitui to the west of Tsavo Park. I told him about my unproductive visit to Machakos. I said perhaps I could return to Kabete through Eastern Province. I certainly had enough to think about. Camels were not the only thing we discussed on the journey, I asked Kasim who with his grey hair was clearly an old man, but I had observed was very active, about his life. He laughed, "I am only half a coastal man. My father was part of a Masai raiding party who reached Mkowe in 1905 the year of the big Rinderpest outbreak in the cattle in Masailand to steal some replacement cattle. I think my mother had a night out like you did last night. I was the result. I am proud of my Masai heritage." He spoke in Swahili. I replied, in my limited Kalenjin, "Your father must have been a very strong man. It is a hell of a long way to walk to Masailand from here."

He replied in Kalenjin, "I have a favour to ask. Can I be your guide and come in your plane to Karawa tomorrow?"

I replied, "I would like that very much."

I had another good night out in Lamu, but I drank less as I would be flying on the next day. I knew my mother and the ladies in Kabete would be appalled that Kasim slept on a blanket beside me on my roof top. He was most respectful, and I was not afraid that he would take advantage of me. He did not snore and hopefully I didn't. I was glad that although he was tall, he was wiry and not a heavy man. I was well aware of the danger he was taking, flying with me.

Mr. Suleiman and his wife waved us goodbye; Benjamin and Saul took us to Manda Island from the Lamu waterfront. Kasim and Benjamin kindly carried the fuel to the microlight, leaving Saul to guard the boat. We were only ten feet above sea level. The runway was long and there were no trees so in fact the take-off was easy and safe. Kasim was not in the least scared and pointed out the landmarks to me on the first leg of our journey above Witu and crossing the Tana at Garsen. We saw the air strip there but did not land. We carried on to a large smooth clearing beside the headquarters of the holding ground at Karawa. We were lucky. Justin the Livestock Officer (LO) from Sabaki holding ground who oversaw Karawa as well, was visiting the staff. We could have a good talk with him about the tsetse survey and possible bush clearing at both holding grounds. He warned us that at Sabaki there were not many tsetse flies but there was a bigger danger to cattle of East Coast Fever (ECF) which was transmitted by ticks, called *Rhipcephalus appendicularis*. I would have to do my homework to find out whether camels could contact ECF. I knew sheep and goats did not.

Kasim left me at Karawa having gripped my hand tightly and telling me in Kalenjin, to take care. Justin promised to get him transport back to Mkowe. I travelled on alone. I saw Sabaki holding ground north of the big Sabaki river. Then I flew by Malindi and its airport before traveling eighty miles to Mombasa airport. I was thankful that I had filled up with petrol at Karawa as my fuel was low on landing. I filled up again at Mombasa. I managed to hitch a lift from a young guy who was learning to fly at Mombasa who was driving back in his car into town. He dropped me at the near end of the causeway which was only 200 yards from the veterinary office.

I walked up to the office with some trepidation. I hoped James Roberton was in a good mood.

He was a changed man. He genuinely seemed to be pleased to see me. I thought it was unlikely to be a view of my breasts which had changed his attitude but more likely because I had solved his problem with the mare. He wanted to hear all about my safari and seemed pleased that I had got some ideas to help solve other problems in his two provinces. He asked me if I would like to stay the night as I must be tired after such a long journey. I had planned to stay with Chris Patten at Miritini, but I thought it would be churlish to refuse his invitation, so at four o'clock I found myself in his car going across the causeway on to Mombasa island. He had the most beautiful house on Tudor creek to the seaward side of the Katherine Bibby hospital. It was a big dwelling and strange because the main living area was upstairs. This was connected by French doors to a big veranda with a romantic view in the moonlight of the dark water behind swaying palm trees. My bedroom was off this veranda. I had a welcome shower and as I had nothing else suitable or clean, put on a simple short, low-cut dress. This seemed to enchant him. Dinner was taken downstairs in a candle lit dining room. His cook was a kikuyu man named Ngonjo. He appreciated my attempts to speak his language much to the amazement of James. After two tuskers, when we were eating mango ice cream with cubes of cut mango which was delicious, I was intoxicated enough to ask him why he was so cross with me when we first met. He did not apologise but said, "I love it here on the coast and I like mixing with people. However, I have this thing about being used as a holiday destination mainly by vets and their families who are based at Kabete or upcountry. I suppose they think that I am a miserable old crabbit because I am never invited back. My really pet hate is young people in their gap year who have somehow got my address from one of my relatives in the UK and then use my house just like a hotel. Somehow, I just equated you with people like them. The way you sorted out that mare showed me that you were not like that."

I certainly had had too many beers as I laughed, "Are you sure it was not the sight of my tits?"

He laughed, "I must admit they are pretty being white and contrasting with the rest of your brown body but what I particularly liked was that they were covered with blood and slim which showed that you were proud to be a practicing vet which sadly I have never been."

I felt sorry for him and realised how lucky I had been enjoying the practicing side of the veterinary profession. I liked his honesty. I was glad we had brought our relationship around. It had been an interesting evening. I was very relaxed when I went to bed. I slept well with the fan clanking away above me. James said I had no need to worry about mosquitos. Of course, I had been taking a malarial prophylactic all the while. In the morning we repaired to his office. His staff were now up to strength. I was introduced in the senior officers room to a middle aged kind, but no nonsense lady who was the Mombasa District Veterinary Officer (DVO), to a young German guy who was the Veterinary Investigation Officer (VIO) for the coast province and, after he had come off the radio, to man from Bungoma District who was a Livestock Officer (LO) for the stock route who mainly worked for the LMD. Together with his Mr. Silas they seemed a happy crowd. They all had some input into my problems in arranging the exportation of healthy camels from Kenya to the Middle East. I took copious notes and thanked them all before James took me to the airport for my onward journey to Machakos. I hoped to over fly the Yatta plateau in Kitui District to get some idea of the terrain for a possible route down to the coast avoiding the tsetse areas, to the main Nairobi-Mombasa Road. I had learnt that morning that because of the wide bush clearance either side of the road the camels would be unlikely to catch trypanosomiasis being lorried down the road. James helped me to tie some extra cans of fuel to the microlight as I planned to land somewhere on the way as Machakos was absolutely at the limit of my range. The wind might help me but gaining four thousand feet would use up rather a lot of fuel. Now I had to see what Tim Stockman the PVO of eastern province would have to say. I wondered if he would be cross that I had not waited to meet him on my previous visit to Machakos.

To my amazement, James hugged me when we parted, and I saw him standing on the tarmac waving me goodbye. The flight went well. I followed the main Mombasa-Nairobi Road for 150 miles and landed at the deserted airfield at Mtito Andei. There I filled up the tank from the cans. These were very light rectangular cans called debbies. They were much sort after by villagers for water transport. I left them on the side of the strip as I knew they would soon be found. As there was no one about, I quickly squatted down for a wee. Then I took off again. I turned north of the road to the Yatta plateau after I had crossed the Athi River. Obviously, I could not really guess whether there were tsetse flies. It looked very barren. There was no evidence of any habitation. I neither saw any game or any cattle. It was a really wild area.

James had said that he would ring Tim to warn him roughly what time I hoped to arrive. It was easy for me to buzz the provincial HQ. I landed on the airstrip into a strong wind. I decided to tie the microlight down to four concrete blocks which had been left on the strip for that purpose. I was busy at my task bending over attaching the ropes when I heard a throat being cleared. I turned rapidly and I was looking at the navel of the PVO Eastern Province. He was enormous. He said, "I'm sorry, I did not mean to alarm you. Let me give you a hand?"

I managed to mumble, "That would be kind."

He continued, "Welcome to Machakos. I am keen on flying as well. I got my Private Pilot's License (PPL) three years ago. The local ranchers are very helpful and allow me to rent their planes. That is much easier that driving into Wilson. Can I be really cheeky and ask you to take me up for a flight sometime?"

I hesitated and blurted out, "I think you would be too heavy."

Mercifully he did not take offence but laughed, "I am not as a heavy as I look. I am under two hundred pounds. You are as light as a feather. I'm sure together we would not weigh more than a normal couple."

I laughed, "I agree that I am not very normal."

He laughed, "Neither am I. I hope you can stay the night."

I replied, "I would love to."

He answered, "Great, the office was closing when I left, we will go straight home for a cup of tea. Then I am due to go rugby training, but as you are here I will skip that."

I asked, "Could I join the training?"

He raised his eyebrows, "That will get the tongues wagging."

I apologised, "I'm sorry. I would not like to get you in trouble with your wife or girlfriend."

He answered, "I have neither. Machakos club has very few eligible young ladies. It's mainly full of rather boring men. So do come training. You look fit. Do you play hockey?"

I responded, "I do but I am away a lot, so I miss lots of games which does not endear me to the captain or the match secretary."

We had reached his Landrover. He asked. "Shall we fill up the microlight. James warned me that you would need some petrol."

I suggested, "Perhaps not, if you want a flight. I am down to about a quarter tank so we will see whether it would be safe in the morning."

He laughed, "No beer for either of us after training then!"

I laughed, "May be just one!"

We got in to the Landrover and he drove the short distance to his house which like other PVO's houses was pretty large. His cook called Hadi, who looked just like Mohamidi Basu, came out to greet us. Tim said, "That's unusual. I hope there is not a drama at the office."

Hadi greeted me in Somali. I returned his greeting in Somali and asked if he was related to Mohamidi. He replied in Somali,

"He is my brother. He spoke very highly of you. He said what a strong woman you are. He said you would make a good wife for this man."

I blushed, "Does he understand Somali?"

Hadi replied, "No he speaks none of my language." He added in Swahili, "Can I take your bag, Memsahib?"

I replied also in Swahili, "Thank you that would be kind. Please don't call me Memsahib. Can you call me Tanya?"

He nodded his head in agreement as Tim said in Swahili, "You have many talents. I guess that you were speaking in Somali."

I replied with a grin also in Swahili, "Yes Hadi was telling me that your PA is his brother."

I hoped Tim had not seen my blush and that he did not understand Somali. I would have been devasted if he had understood as I had to admit that I did fancy him even though he was a giant.

We had a quick cup of tea before we left to go to the club for rugby training. I enjoyed it. The other men seemed to accept me after Tim had made the introductions. Of course, I had difficulty remembering all the names as there were eleven of them. We started with a few exercises and then started doing things with a ball. I was used to handling a rugby ball from my days at vet school and in the garden at home with my brother. I wondered when it would ever be acceptable for girls to play rugby. I really could not see why girls couldn't play. I thought mixed hockey was much more dangerous.

I asked Tim when we were going back to his house without having a shower whether I had embarrassed him. He replied reassuringly, "Not at all. I often leave as I actually take my job quite seriously. I don't want to get involved in a drinking session and have a sore head in the morning."

I said, "You are quite young to be a PVO. I guess that you are a rising star in the department."

He answered, "I am amazed that you got your job being young and female!"

I did not lie to him but told him how I had tricked ODA. I begged him not to tell anyone and he promised he wouldn't.

We had showers when we got to his home. I had my own en suite bathroom. Hadi did us proud with his cooking for our supper. I expected that we would look at maps after dinner, but we didn't. Tim put on a LP on the gramophone. After we had had a cup of coffee and Hadi had said good night. I was very bold and asked if we could dance. I knew it was very forward of me, but I just felt like being in a man's arms. Tim did not seem to mind. I apologised for my small stature, but he made light of it saying that he did not expect me to bring a ball gown and high heels when I went on safari.

When he was changing the record, he casually asked if I would come with him to the Muthaiga Club ball a week on Saturday. I said I would love to and that I hoped he would stay with me at Kabete. He said he had a rugby game at Nondescripts on Saturday afternoon so that would fit in very well.

We weren't late to bed. I thought how lucky we were to have our own houses. I would have found asking a guy to stay in my old flat above the branch surgery very difficult in the UK. Going out with a group of boys had been easy at vet college but was not easy when one started work. Also, out here to some extent I was my own boss. I did not have to be on call the whole time.

I teased Tim as we had a fry-up for breakfast. I said we would never get the microlight into the air if he wanted a flight. I was pleased he was a pilot. It gave us another thing in common. I thought that I might start to get my PPL as that would give me more versatility. The microlight was rather restrictive.

I shook Hadi by the hand and thanked him for my stay. On the way to the office. I asked Tim's advice as to whether I should have given Hadi a tip. I had not tipped Ngonjo in Mombasa. Tim said that he was never sure what to do. He said he always did give a tip if he was away playing rugby or if he was on local leave. However, he did not normally give a tip if he was staying somewhere when he was working. He said years ago in his gap year he had been travelling in Australia. There, you never gave a tip even in a restaurant. Australians thought that it was belittling to give a tip. Here the wages were so small he thought it was different. He laughed and said that actually Hadi had a good deal as Tim did not think he was very demanding. Tim said he was appalled how badly some wives treated their servants. I said that I hoped I had a good relationship with Matua and was not too demanding. I laughed and said that it had horrified me that he had ironed my knickers when I first arrived, but that now I accepted that as normal. This seemed to amuse Tim.

When we got to the office it was all business. I was introduced to the DVO and the DLO after I had greeted Mohamidi. Then we were huddled together looking at maps. I was rather sad that there was no inappropriate touching. In fact, Tim had rather bad news. He said that trying to cross the Yatta Plateau with camels would be very difficult, not only in the rains when the steep paths would very treacherous and slippery, but also in the dry weather when the camels would cut their feet. Apart from that he knew the bush beside the Athi River was full of tsetse flies and he thought that certainly the bush north of the Yatta Plateau beside the Tiva River was likely to harbour tsetse flies, as well. He suggested that perhaps a way could be found to bring the camels down from the Tana River through the land owned by The Orma Tribe to the Sabaki River and then beside Tsavo Game Park to Mackinnon Road on the main Nairobi/Mombasa Road. However, he said that this would require a large amount of bush clearing and regular spraying.

He did end by saying with a grin that he would try to think of other excuses to get me to visit him. He said he was sad that he had not helped me during my camel census in Marsabit District.

We had coffee with the rest of the staff before he drove me out to the airstrip. I had done my arithmetic and I thought that it would be safe for us to have a flight as I was not carrying much fuel. So, leaving my limited luggage in his Landrover we got strapped in. I liked the feel of his hands on my shoulders. I was rather hoping that he would stroke my neck, but he didn't. We trundled down the long runway with the wind. We turned at the far end. I pushed the throttle to full power, and we were off. I felt his hands tense on my shoulders. He had no need to be concerned. We took off with no problems. He shouted in my ear, "This is exciting. I am glad it is a beautiful day. We get a lot of low stratus here, particularly in July and August," He stroked my neck and shouted, "You will have to come to stay in your Landrover then." I was delighted. Our attraction seemed to be mutual. The DVS had been correct.

I did not take him for too long a sight-seeing tour because I was worried about the fuel. Also, I knew that he would know the area well. I shouted, "Did you get your PPL at Wilson?"

He replied, "Yes, I did. It is quite scary as there are so many aircraft in the circuit which is an unusual one being right-handed. You have got Eastleigh and Embakasi to contend with."

I asked, "Do you think I could manage it? I think that the authorities will soon clamp down on strange craft like this. I have no license. I just got in and flew it."

He replied, "Of course you could. I think you could do anything. You will probably be the first women to play rugby for Kenya!"

I shouted, "I wish!"

We turned into land. I shouted, "I'm sorry I can't let you land as it is not like a plane it does not have dual control."

I heard him laugh, "I'll stick to proper planes."

We landed. He gave me a hug to thank me for his trip. Then we filled up the tank from two cans from his Landrover. I strapped in my luggage, and I was off, with him shouting, "See you a week on Saturday. Take care."

Chapter 8

I was quite excited about the coming weekend. Matua kindly made up one of the spare rooms and put some towels out. I decided to watch the rugby game, so I put on a short skirt and went on my motorbike. The players were warming up on the pitch. Tim must have seen me as he ran over. I was a little surprised, but delighted when he gave me a kiss on my lips and then said, "I like the view of your legs, but are you safe on that thing?"

I replied, "I hope you are worried about the state of the roads and are not being rude about girl drivers. I've come to cheer you on."

He answered, "I'm delighted you have come to watch. I am just worried about your modes of transport. First the microlight and now a motorbike. Machakos have only got two other families supporting us. Come on I will introduce you."

Grabbing my hand, we run like school kids to the side of the pitch. I meet Joan and Rachael who seem to have a large number of kids who are tearing around totally out of control. Tim goes on to the pitch to join his teammates.

I pick up a ball and shout to the children, "Who wants to join me for a game?" The kids are intrigued as they are not used to grown-ups paying them any attention out of school. They follow me as I run to a second pitch to the side of the club house. I separate them into two teams, and they are soon playing a game of touch rugby. The girls seem really keen. I keep them occupied for about twenty minutes before we all go over to watch the match which has been in progress for several minutes. Rachael has a cool bag and gives them bottles of Coca-Cola with straws. I am included. Joan turns to me, "Thanks for doing that. It is good to have a break from the little horrors. They don't all belong to Rachael and me. There are three other families. Are you a schoolteacher?"

I reply, "No I'm a vet."

Rachael says, "Well you are marvellous with them. Do you work with Tim?"

I answer, "Yes, but he is very senior to me."

Joan giggles, "You work under him?"

I reply, raising my bottle, "I'm ever hopeful."

Rachael said, "If the kiss he gave you when you arrived is anything to go by, I think you will get lucky. He was dumped by a girl who went off to the UK. I think it hit him rather hard." As far as I know he has never taken out another girl."

The conversation stopped as the play came over to our side of the pitch. It was obvious that Nondescripts were a more practiced team, but Machakos were stronger players as individuals. Tim was in the thick of it. He was obviously the leader of the pack. He could have been the captain. I shouted, "Come on Machakos. Let's have a try."

The play moved away. Rachael said, "You obviously understand the game."

I replied, "I do. My older brother plays in England, as did my father."

Rachael asked, "Do you play any sport."

I answered, "Hockey, Squash and Tennis when I can. I am away rather a lot in the NFD looking after camels.

Rachael said, "That must be rather lonely."

I smiled, "I have made lots of friends up there." I knew that she wanted to ask me more but was nervous because it was not normal for young, unmarried girls to be friendly with Africans."

I enjoyed watching the game. Equally I was glad that I had not been playing hockey as I rather wanted to save myself for the ball. I knew that I would be dancing until the early hours. As it was, I had a near death experience which because I had had several drinks I found idiotically amusing.

I, like all the ladies was wearing a long dress. Mine was low-cut and had a slit up the left-hand side nearly to the top of my thigh. I thought it was sexy. Certainly, Tim seemed to think it was. What he was not aware of was that I had not bothered with any underwear at all. He had followed me home after the game. We then had plenty of time to bath and change. He congratulated me in not having a handbag when I asked him to put my purse and my lipstick in the pocket of his dinner jacket.

The dinner, which was in a marquee, interrupted by dances was good fun. It was after dinner when things got rather out of hand. Some of the men climbed up to the top of the outside of the marquee and started a sort of jousting type of wrestling match. I decided to join them. This was neither sensible because I was much smaller than them, nor demure as I was showing a lot of bare leg. I did not know that the short guy I was competing against was the best polo player in the country. He was very strong, and he did not just topple me by threw me up and out on to the sloping canvass.

I somersaulted down falling the last eight feet on to the grass. They say babies and drunkards fall light. I must have been drunk! I did not hurt myself. As I got to my feet, I realised that I had landed within two feet of a big metal peg which was holding up the marquee. I had been lucky.

From then on, I stuck to dancing. Tim was a good dancer and surprisingly we danced well together considering our very different heights, even with my high heels. Some of the time we were energetic, but I was sure that he enjoyed the slow numbers as much as me.

Wisely we opted to go home at 3.00 am. Many did not. I could see there was going to be some serious drinking until dawn. Tim seemed quite sober when he drove us to my house. I was standing by the sideboard pouring us pints of cold water from a big jug which I had got from the refrigerator. He came up behind me and kissed my neck. Then he reached over and slipped his right hand inside my dress on to my bare breast. He reached up the slit in my gown and murmured into my ear, "You are a very naughty girl."

The phone went. I said, "Dam."

He groaned, "You had better answer it. Anyone one ringing at this hour must think that it is important."

I broke away from him and did as he suggested. It was the DVS, "I'm sorry to bother you Tanya at this late hour, but I have a crisis on my hands. I have had a message from the High Commission. They have had information from the Ethiopian Government. There is an outbreak of what they think is Rinderpest north of the Dawa River near to a village called Rhama on our side of the border."

I replied, "I know the place."

He answered, "I guessed you might. I have discussed the issue with James, and he thought that you would help us out by flying up there to investigate."

I said, "I will leave at first light. I will carry extra fuel and land at Garba Tulla to fill up the microlight's tank. Can you arrange that Axmeed, the DLO at Wajir meets me at the airstrip with fuel and water when I buzz him, as that could be my next fuel stop. I will report on the veterinary frequency on the hour to keep James informed. Can you clear my safari with Neils."

He replied, "I'm not sure where those places are but I will look on the map. Good luck. Take care."

That was that. I turned into Tim's arms. He asked almost pleading, "Can't I fly you up?"

I answered, "You could. It would have been fun, but the DVS is a cunning old fox. He won't want to pay to hire a plane. Even as a PVO you will get into big trouble. I will get word to you if I have a problem. However, if you can help me with the microlight. I am wide awake now."

He wrapped me in his arms, and we kissed passionately. I really wanted a cuddle. However, the moment was lost.

We must have woken Matua. I know he would have left us alone if we had been in bed. He came through with mugs of tea and said that he would make us breakfast after I told him what was going on. Tim and I chatted away after we had changed out of our smart clothes. I put on a sweater as it was quite chilly.

It was the middle of the afternoon when I was fifteen minutes out of Rhama. I could see the vultures wheeling on the other side of the river. I could not see any on the Kenya side. I also could not see any cattle south of the river. I guessed that the rumour of the plague had reached the villagers and they had moved their cattle south out of danger. I just hoped that they had not taken the disease with them. I landed and filled up the microlights tank with fuel. Then I walked into the village. I knew there was not a shop. I could only find some elderly Boran people. Luckily one old man could understand my Swahili. He told me all the cattle on this side of the river were now a long way away. He walked with me to the river. He said that it was not deep, and he laughed saying I would not have to swim.

I felt a real trollop walking across the river naked except for my gym shoes, with my sample-taking box on my head. There was no one with the dead cattle. Most of them were dead. I took some blood from the jugulars from two moribund animals. I wished I had my gun to put them out of their misery. I looked in their mouths. I was certain that it was rinderpest. I took samples from the lesions in their mouths. I cut into one of the freshly dead ones. It had the tell-tailed zebra-stripe marking in its rectum. I remembered the film that they had shown us at vet school. It was definitely rinderpest.

I waded back across and thanked the old man for his help. He seemed to know all about me. I thought what a strange girl, I was. I was not the least bit shy drying my body with my shirt before putting on my shorts while he calmly watched me. I hoped that I would not be shy in front of Tim.

I managed to get back to Wajir just before dark. I had kept my word and had faithfully reported on each hour. I had only had one acknowledgement on the way up. It was my friend Mr. Suleiman. Obviously, Sunday was like any other day to him. I promised to come up to visit him if I got the chance. I wondered if I could fly up with Tim. Lamu was such a romantic place. I imagined the two of us together but otherwise alone under the palm trees on the east of the island.

By dusk I was absolutely shattered. I had supper with Axmeed before getting a good night's sleep. I took off again at first light remembering to bring the samples which had been in the veterinary fridge overnight. Once again, I transferred fuel at Gaba Tulla on an empty airstrip. When I next called up, James came on. He thanked me profusely for all my efforts. He had already heard that I was certain that it was Rinderpest. He had got together with the ADVS (Field), John Adams. A massive vaccination was going to be carried out very soon. Starting in Mandera. I hoped I might be able to get together with Tim because I thought after Mandera District, Marsabit District would be the next on the list. Of course, Marsabit District came under Tim.

I was once again totally exhausted when I landed at lower Kabete. However, I just had a quick cup of tea with Matua before I got on my motorbike and went up to the Vet Labs. They were just closing the diagnostic lab but they stayed open and started processing my samples before I went up to see the DVS. The DDVS, ADVS (Field) and ADVS (Lab) joined us. They were gobsmacked by my journey.

When they heard that I had been doing post-mortems on dead cattle in Ethiopia in the nude you could have heard a pin drop. I think they were worried about an international incident, but it might have been them imagining me naked which caused the hush.

I went home to have a nourishing supper which Matua had prepared and then I crashed into bed and slept for thirteen hours. The following day I was rung by the DVS to tell me that my samples had confirmed Rinderpest he thanked me once again and said he would keep me up to date with developments. His underlying message was clear that now I should concentrate on my camels. Neils and I had a long discussion. We both felt that we needed to get a boat load of camels to act as a trial or the FAO/UN would give up on us. At least camels did not get rinderpest.

Dick White managed to get a buyer who wanted two hundred camels and two hundred large steers, to sell in Aden. This was good from the point of view that together they would fill the vessel. It was not good because of the rinderpest. However, we might get away with it if the rinderpest remained north of our border. I would just have to hope that the veterinary department expedited the vaccination campaign. It certainly was in every one's best interest.

I thought Dick White would have no problem providing us with the cattle. However, I was wrong. He said he would have no difficulty purchasing the camels as there was a surplus in the NFD. He said, because of the booming tourist trade there was a shortage of prime cattle. Chris Patten came to my rescue. He had a mob of 300 cattle which were ready for slaughter. They were grazing on Taita land near to Mackinnon Road. He knew they included some heifers, but he thought he could find 200 steers.

Dick White kindly came down with me on the train to Mombasa. We picked up Chris on our way through Miritini having borrowed a Landrover with James's permission from the Mombasa Veterinary Office. We selected 200 steers. Dick valued them and a sale was agreed. The deal included Chris looking after to them until they were loaded on to a ship in

Kilindini Harbour. It saved Dick hiring herdsmen for what we hoped would be only a short time.

Dick and I called in and had a cup of tea with James. He was sad that we were returning on the overnight train and therefore could not stay the night with him. I promised to come to stay when I came down again to load the animals on to the boat. Because they were local cattle from the Coast Province, James knew that they were all vaccinated against rinderpest, and free of FMD and CBPP.

I flew Dick up to Isiolo where he bought the camels. I had given up the idea of trying to trek them down to the coast and so Dick said that he would hire lorries to carry them to the railhead at Nanyuki. Then they could go by rail via Nairobi direct to the docks in Kilindini harbour.

Now I had to hire a boat. I had to smile as it seemed the bigger the mode of transport, the easier it was to procure it. Trying to hire a car was not easy. Tim on the other hand had no problems hiring an aircraft. I had no problem hiring a boat. I did it on the telephone using an agent named Mathew Clarkson who worked for an import/export firm called Smith Mackenzie. The boat would arrive in Mombasa in three days' time. It would take two days to off load its cargo of steel. I would then have a week to refit it with pens to accommodate the animals. Although I would have enjoyed having a week staying with James on the coast, Neils agreed to do this task while I travelled up the Nanyuki to load the camels and travel down with them via Nairobi to Mombasa. Percy Gibbons helped me to hire Samburu men to load the camels and then travel down with them. A Nanyuki farmer called Reg Pertwee who I had met at Nanyuki Sports Club sold me enough forage to feed the camels and the cattle for the whole journey not only on the train, but also on the ship.

Dick had managed to get two buyers from Aden, one to buy the cattle and the other to buy the camels. Dick hired a plane to take them to Nanyuki and then down to Mombasa, where they were met by Chris and taken the short journey of fifty miles on a tarmac road to Mackinnon Road. These buyers had permits itemising the veterinary requirements and handling instructions for me. The whole organisation became a complete nightmare. It was completely outside of, not only my comfort zone, but also outside of the sadly rather limited experience of Neils.

It did have some humorous aspects. The Samburu camel-herders were very knowledgeable about herding camels but little else. The fact that I spoke some of their language and was travelling with them and the camels seemed strange to them. Samburu girls were expected to herd sheep and goats with Samburu boys until puberty. Then the boys went on to herd cattle and eventually the chosen men became camel herders. The girls were married and had families. I was a girl who they could see had reached puberty but had not married and now somehow was a camel herder. They found it easier to pretend that I was a man. I was treated very respectfully as a headman together with another man, Kiptoung who was in his prime and was also a headman. We were expected to do everything together. Thank goodness I was not shy when it came to washing and abluting. When we were just with the camels it was relatively straightforward, it was like being the only girl in a rugby changing room. The problems came when I had to deal with Europeans. My thoughts often drifted back to the cowshed in Wiltshire. At least here I was warmer, although the journey from Nanyuki to Nairobi was cold at night What my mother would have said about me lying down with twenty men just wrapped in red blankets did not bear thinking about. Kiptoung kindly found me a red blanket. I really felt 'one of the lads.'

The nights slowly became warmer as we lost altitude after Nairobi. My journey was quite restful. Kiptoung and I were not expected to any heavy work. One camel had a septic wound on its leg from an accident when it was loaded in Nanyuki. This needed cleaning and covered with oily cream twice a day. I learnt a lot more of their language. This became very important when we arrived in Kilindini Docks. Neils had done a first-class job making pens below decks which from our instructions from Aden, were for the camels, and on the top deck for the cattle.

We loaded the fodder first below decks and then went to load the camels. There was no way they were going down the chute into the dark hole. They immediately went into the kush position and then there was no shifting them. The herdsmen tried shouting. I stopped the herdsmen using sticks or camel whips as the welfare aspects appalled me. We tried putting blindfolds on them but that did not work. In desperation we tried loaded the cattle down on to the lower decks. They were no problem and happily walked down the chute. Then to all our surprise when we tried to load the camels on to the upper decks, we had no problems. They walked on as if they were going on holiday. There was a large amount of slapping of hands together before the Samburu men boarded the railway truck to take them back to Nanyuki where Dick had said he would get them back by lorry to Isiolo.

Then the shit hit the fan. The buyers from Aden arrived with their men to go on the boat to look after their animals on the voyage. When they saw the camels on the upper decks in the fresh air. They started shouting and waving their arms. They directed all their abuse at me. The sea air would make all the camels die. Had I not been instructed to load the camels below decks. Of course, I had. I could not deny I had seen the instructions. I explained carefully what lengths that we had gone to, to try to load the camels, but they would not have that. I so wished that I had left with the friendly Samburu. The captain of the ship tried to help me. He wanted to set sail. Every hour he was tied up on the dock was costing money. He would even have to pay if he was anchored in the harbour. I managed to track down Mathew Clarkson. By now it was dark. There was no way that I was going to let them off load the animals and then try to reload them again. I could imagine the drama if the cattle escaped on the harbour wall. Mathew arrived and after some considerable amount of haggling he agreed to refund some of the buyer's money. The ship then sailed. I thought, 'Thank goodness for that'. Chris Patten took me back to his home. One benefit was that I had a lovely ride out with him in the morning. I did some sunbathing in the afternoon and he put me on the train to return to Nairobi overnight.

Neils and I now had a problem. The trial of exporting the camels had been a financial disaster. We sat in our office trying to think how we would proceed. I had been in touch with Dick. He did his best to help us. With his one-line vote he could move funds about so that it would look to the Kenyan Government that the export of the 200 cattle had broken even. However, there was still a massive loss when it came to the camels. FAO was not happy. Neils had finished his contract. He had been seconded by the Norwegian Government. He was due leave at the end of his contract. He left to take the leave and then he would return to his previous job with the Norwegian Government.

I had a month before my contract ended. I longed to go and see Tim and ask his advice. However, he seemed to be permanently on safari in Marsabit District. He had not been permitted to fly as the Ministry of Agriculture who had overall control of the financial budget for the Veterinary Department would not pay for flying. I gathered he had managed to come back to Machakos for a weekend in a Police-Airwing plane but I had been away dealing with the camels and so we had not seen one another.

I felt our night out had been a success. I thought sadly that he might not think the same. Now I was twiddling my thumbs with nothing to do. To cheer myself up. I did a lot of running, I trained with the Hockey girls twice a week and got picked to play on Saturdays. I spent my time in the office writing up the project report. More importantly I managed to draw some results from our tick surveys, and the bloods which we had collected to write two papers which I hoped eventually would be published in the Veterinary Record. I was dreading returning to the UK. I had fallen in love with Kenya. I had made many friends. I had not found a man, but I knew that I was much more likely to find one here than in England.

Mercifully Rinderpest had not spread into Kenya. I suspected that was because of the hard work being put in by the field vets, livestock officers and veterinary scouts in the NFD. Unbeknown to me others thought differently. I was sitting in our office having just received the official confirmation that our project was being closed down. The only good thing was that all the equipment and the vehicles including the microlight was being handed over to the Kenyan Government. I was summoned to go to see the DVS.

To my surprise, he greeted me affably, "Sit down Tanya. I have never thanked you properly for your marvellous job confirming the Ethiopian Rinderpest outbreak. You will now be aware that your project has ended. I wondered what your plans were?"

I replied, "I was just reading the official confirmation that the whole project is going to be closed down. I had expected it, but I'm pretty gloomy. The last thing I want to do is to return to the UK."

He smiled, "I thought that might be the case. I would like to offer you a job at least for three months. Would you be interested?"

I hesitated, "I am very grateful, but it depends on the job. I'm not really happy stuck in an office or a laboratory."

He smiled, "Even if it allowed you to play hockey regularly?"

I also smiled, "I can't say I don't enjoy playing but I need more in my life than that."

He continued, "Well, I have a problem, James is due to go on three and half months leave. As you are aware, North Eastern province comes under him. The Mombasa vets would be able to manage the majority of the work on Mombasa Island, and in Kwale, Kilifi and Taita Districts. John Adams ADVS (Field) could supervise the DLOs in Tana River and Lamu Districts thanks to your introduction of radios. However, with this risk of rinderpest I would like someone to really be in charge. Would you accept forgoing your leave and stand in as an acting capacity as PVO for James. He, like me, thinks that you are quite capable of the post."

I answered with no hesitation, "I would jump at the chance, Sir."

He replied good, "I cannot guarantee you overseas terms, but I will try to get them for you. I can guarantee you four months local salary as a PVO."

I said, "Thank you, I have just one request. Can I be issued with the microlight?"

He chuckled, "Certainly provide you promise me to take care of yourself and not take any unnecessary risks."

That was it. My first job was to ask Matua if he would come with me to the coast. He would be a long way from his family. Matua sounded very relaxed. He said if he could have just two weeks leave to go home and then, if he could take money for the rest of leave as that would be more useful to him. It was ideal. He could come down with my stuff with Stanley and Morton after he had the two weeks leave. I got a note from the DVS asking me if I would like to take the motorbike. This was really kind of him as it would save me buying a car. I had saved some money in Kenya and all my UK earnings, so I was not poor. However, I knew that I would want to buy a house in the UK eventually and so if I invested the money carefully, buying government stocks whose interest did not accrue a tax liability, as I was working abroad, I would have something to fall back on. I was well aware that I was not entitled to any pension.

Although I was pleased to have at least the next three months of my life sorted out, I was a little sad to leave my house which

I loved. I knew Beaver would like to go to the coast. He loved swimming. I also would miss the hockey girls, but I planned to keep playing in Mombasa. I admitted to myself that I was sad that now Tim and I would be very far apart and that our relationship was not likely to blossom. Naturally I did not say anything to anyone one else. I still imagined the feel of his hand on my breast as I was washing myself or lying in bed.

I flew the microlight down the 320 miles to Mombasa. The Mombasa flying club kindly let me leave it in their hanger as I said that I would probably like to try and get my PPL when I got settled. Stanley and Morton brought the motorbike down in the Landrover with my belongings. There was a shed at the back of the PVO's house where I could keep it. It was the custom that an incoming officer spent ten days with the outgoing officer to affect a proper handover. James kindly let me stay with him although I was entitled to stay in a hotel or in the club. I took James out for a meal at the 'Mombasa Club' which because it was down near the water in Tudor Creek was nicknamed, 'The Chini Club'. (Chini means below in Swahili). I checked that it was OK for me to use the club as it reciprocated with the Nanyuki Sports Club. Dick White had given me good advice about joining the Nanyuki Sports Club as it also reciprocated with Mombasa Sports Club where I could play Hockey and Squash. I joined the Water Ski Club as I wanted to get better at water-skiing. It was ideal that it was withing easy walking distance and indeed swimming distance of the PVO's house. There was nothing more refreshing to go down have a quick ski with Sealion driving after work before going home for supper.

I had supper one night with Angela and Alan Barret. They volunteered to propose me for the sailing club. However, I said that I would think about it. The atmosphere at the Sailing Club was rather stuffy and I thought that I would probably not sail very often.

James went on leave and his cook left to go upcountry to take his leave. Matua settled in and soon was doing all the shopping and in fact everything else about the house. I loved the upstairs veranda where I would sit out in the dark and watch the stars and moon come out. I just wished I had a man's arms around me.

The DVS had been correct. I had little to do in the Mombasa office and the neighbouring districts. So, I decided to leave Beaver with Matua and visit Tana River District and Lamu District before going the Garissa. I got a very welcoming arrival on Lamu Island. I spent a whole day on the mainland with Mr Suleman and so I returned with him to spend a second night at Petley's Hotel. Kasim and I were firm friends and so he joined us for an enjoyable evening in the bar. There was no surprise for me that I had fish curry both nights. On the way up I had visited Sabaki and Karawa Holding grounds as well as the small veterinary office at Garsen which was on the South Side of the Tana River. There was a ferry which operated across the river during the dry season. The head veterinary scout Daniel Toya at Garsen said that he was concerned that there were cattle which grazed along the south bank of the river illegally in the holding ground and that they had never been vaccinated against rinderpest, mainly because there was not access to them by road.

I remembered the rubber boat at Lamu. I persuaded Mr. Suleiman and Kasim to join Daniel and I on a safari in the boat down the river. It was quite a hair-raising experience, as with the extra fuel we needed, we were a little over loaded. There were plenty of crocodiles but what was much scarier was the hippos. They would be lying on a sandbank. When we came around the corner, they would all dive into the water. We very nearly got swamped on two occasions. We saw three villages. We stopped and went ashore. Sure, enough there were cattle not showing the Z brand of rinderpest vaccination.

It was getting dark when we eventually reached the mouth of the river. Karissa, The Lamu driver was there waiting for us.

While the others were loading up the rubber boat. Daniel and I went to see the District Officer at the small village of Kipini. He agreed to help Daniel to build crushes and to get the cattle presented for vaccination. All in all, it was a worthwhile visit. I was sure we were entitled to another night out at Petley's before I set off for Galole to see the DLO and then on to Garissa.

There was a lot of activity at the veterinary office at Garissa. The rinderpest campaign had been completed in Madera and Wajir Districts. They were now finishing up in Garissa District. Both the DVO and the DC seemed pleased that vets from Kabete were showing an interest. They took me to the PC who in far flung places like Garissa only really reports to God. He was a jovial man and welcomed me to a goat stew for lunch. I then flew on to spend the night at Wajir.

There was good news in Wajir. Not only had they finished the vaccination campaign, but they had scoured the water holes and villages and could not find any evidence that there was any rinderpest in the district. There was similar good news in Mandera. I took my life in my hands and had a flight up the Dawa River. There were no vultures wheeling in the sky. It certainly looked as if the outbreak of disease had died out.

I spent the night at Mandera and then took off at dawn to fly to El Wak. I flew along the Somalian border, but in Kenya. I knew just how dangerous it was. I was just desperate to reassure myself that there was no rinderpest near to Kenya. It was very foolish. One second, I was flying at two hundred feet straight and level. The next second, Woosh. I was rocking about totally out of control being pushed down to the ground. I was terrified. I knew not to turn, or I would lose more height. I flew straight and managed to stabilise myself and turn ninety degrees to my right heading directly into Kenya away from Somalia.

The Somali jet was not satisfied. He buzzed me again. The shock wave somehow rebounded off the ground and threw me not only upwards, but also upside down. I will never know how

I survived. I must have done an inverted loop to get the microlight flying the correct way up and then I was crashing through the acacia bush at a horrendous speed. I came to rest and smelt petrol fumes. I had the presence of mind to snap open my harness jump to the ground and run. Then I was thrown on to my face by the blast as the fuel tank exploded. However, I was alive, and I got groggily to my feet and stumbled further away from the blazing wreck.

I watched the victorious jet fly off to the east. I followed a cattle track in the same direction. In about half an hour I reached the Mandera/El Wak Road. I turned and trudged wearily south along the road. Mercifully although the sun was up it was not blazing with heat, and I made good progress. I had absolutely nothing, no water, no food. I had even lost my pocket compass which must have been ripped off my neck. My watch was still around my wrist, but it was smashed. I smiled as I took it off. I could not be in too bad a shape, as I was still worried about getting a tan mark.

It seemed like hours, but I think it was only about two when I was sure that I could see the fort at El Wak. I walked with more purpose as it slowly got bigger. The DO was very kind and helpful. He quickly got a message through to Wajir that I was safe and well. Within a couple of hours, a veterinary department Landrover arrived from Wajir, and I was transported southwards, first to Wajir and then on to Garissa. There to my amazement was Mr. Suleman and Kasim. They had heard of my disaster and had come to collect me. It was the middle of the night by the time I was eating a fish curry and drinking a cold beer with Peter and Darki. I got a lift the following day on the Bonanza with a load of cattle destined for the abattoir in Mombasa. The captain kindly hove to, opposite my house on Tudor Creek so that I could dive off the boat and swim to my house. I received an exuberant welcome from Beaver and Matua.

Chapter 9

The morning was rather an anti-climax. There was the normal round up on the radio. When I got into the office I rang John Adams, my immediate superior, to tell him the good news that there was no evidence of any rinderpest in Kenya and that we would of course finish the vaccination campaign in Garissa District. He already knew that we had finished the campaign in Tana River and Lamu Districts. He said nothing about my crash. I was surprised that no word of it had reached Kabete. Then I thought why should it have had? It wasn't as if the Somalis would have been boasting to the Kenyan Government to claim that they had downed a microlight over Kenyan Airspace. I got Mr. Silas to fill in the normal forms as if I had crashed and written off a Landrover. Karissa, the Mombasa driver drove me up to Mombasa Airport to retrieve my motorbike. I went to the flying club hanger to tell them about my disaster and get the motor bike. I was about to drive away when I looked over to the terminal.

There was Tim with a very striking, leggy blond getting into a taxi. They had obviously just flown down on the morning Nairobi flight. Now I knew why he had not contacted me. I was tired and I burst into tears. I just sat astride the motorbike. Then I thought, 'Tanya don't be so bloody wet. You hardly knew the man. He has every right to take another girl off for some leave on the beach.' I dried my eyes and got off the bike. I walked back into the flying club and enrolled to learn to fly with a view to getting my PPL. They gave me the name and address in Mombasa of the doctor who was officially licensed to take flying medicals. I booked up my first lesson for the following morning at 6.45 am. I would then be easily on time for the office as it was on this side of the causeway. Brian the instructor who worked for the water department said it was a good time to start as there was no wind early in the mornings. This made it easier for beginners. He also said it suited him as he needed to get to his office by 8.00 am.

I drove to the doctor, and he gave me the medical there and then. He laughed, "I like doing medicals because I put the fee straight in my pocket and don't have to put it through the books and pay any income tax. I don't examine many girls. What's your job?"

I replied, "I'm a vet."

Then I had to hear everything about his dog that had broken its tooth catching a stick and bled all over his car. I passed my medical in record time. I flew with Brian every week-day morning that week. On the Friday he let me go solo, I was scared but also delighted. I loved flying and had transitioned from microlights to standard fixed wing planes without any difficulty. I did my two mandatory cross-country trips without problems. Normally you do the first one with your instructor, but Brian let me do them both on my own as I had done so much navigating already. I used them for government business visiting cattle at Voi and at Lamu. I could log the hours which naturally I had to pay for. However, I could easily claim the mileage as if I had been using my own vehicle even though I did not have one. It was very cost effective. I wondered if Tim knew that he could do that. I often thought of him. I had the lovely legs of the blond etched in my brain.

The written exam for my PPL was a doddle. I had learnt a large amount about navigation, air law and radiotelephony in the last two years. I was nervous about my flying test, but Brian said provided I concentrated I would pass. I did concentrate and I did pass. I had several beers at the water-ski club that evening to celebrate.

Water skiing was so cheap, and I had done a lot in the past two and a half months. I was totally at home on a mono-ski and could come through the slalom course at considerable speed. A visiting naval supply ship, HMS Triumph had made us a water ski-jump, to thank us all for letting the crew spend time at the club. After several spectacular crashes I had mastered jumping and now could jump over seventy feet. It was very exhilarating. I was determined to master one more skill before my time at the coast ended. That was to ski barefoot. You needed to be light which I was. You needed to be athletic which I hoped I was and finally you had to be courageous, as the boat needed to be going at over thirty-five miles an hour. With Sealion driving, when there was no one else about I tried to master the skill.

Now I could easily start wearing a single ski very loose on my left foot. Sealion would slowly build up the speed. I would be in a crouch position sticking up my bottom up into the air in a very unlady-like manner. With my elbows tucked into my tummy I had to put my bare right foot into the water and transfer my weight on to it before kicking the mono-ski off and transferring the weight back on to both feet. Several evenings I tried and tried to manage the procedure, nearly drowning myself in the process. At last, I accomplished it. I managed a complete circuit of the big area in the creek on bare feet.

I still was not satisfied. I had read in an American magazine that guys in the states now started bare foot skiing by starting in the water lying on their backs with their legs hooked over the rope. The driver increased the speed and they aquaplaned on their backs. When they were going fast enough. They flipped up on to their feet and they were skiing on their bare feet. I gave up wearing a bikini as I was always losing my top. Not that I was worried about that as I knew Sealion was not fussed. I wore a one-piece lycra swimming costume. I thought I looked very sexy. The only downside was that it was not fun waxing.

I was delighted as I managed to flip up on a regular basis before my time at the coast had ended. I spent ten fun days with James carrying out our hand over before I set off to Kabete to find out what the DVS had planned for me. I dumped my stuff in our old store and released Matua to go to see his family. I went to see the DVS.

He seemed delighted to see me. I expected some sort of reprimand for writing off the microlight. It was not mentioned so I kept quiet. He said he was pleased that he had got me on to overseas terms and so I would be getting my overseas allowance which was very welcome. I anticipated that I would revert to a VO's salary, but he assured me he had a better plan if I was happy to be flexible. He explained his problem.

He had six PVOs and one ADVS in the field. At any one time he had one of them on leave for three months. If I accepted, he wanted me to move between provinces and take over from the PVOs and even the ADVS who was based in the biggest province, The Rift Valley, when they each went on leave every two years. He saw my grimace when I thought about spending three months in Kisumu the HQ of Nyanza Province and in Kakamega, the HQ of Western Province. He tried to encourage me by saying that I would get a better salary than an ordinary PVO as I would be acting ADVS when I was in Rift Valley Province and of course when I was doing the ADVS Field job here at Kabete. When I thought about it, I realised that it was ideal for me. I could do plenty of water skiing on Lake Victoria when I was in Kisumu and there was a thriving club in Kitali, where I could play hockey, tennis, and squash, which was near to Kakamega. He was delighted when I smiled and said that I was pleased to accept his kind offer.

The DVS said, "That is a real relief for me as Tim goes on leave in a couple of weeks. You with your flying will be able to make a hundred percent certain that rinderpest does not come in to Marsabit District from Ethiopia. It seemed to work out very well, you staying with James for the handover in Mombasa. I was so glad you sorted out your differences. He was full of praise for you when he came through Kabete at the end of his leave."

My mind was in a complete whirl when I left his office. How could I stay with Tim, with the blond in residence? I supposed that I could commute from Nairobi for ten days. There might even be a government rest house in Machakos where I could stay. I got a Landrover and a driver out of the vehicle pool at Kabete. I only had the motorbike and my clothes and, my personal things. I could easily get them into a Landrover in the same way that they had come up to Kabete from Mombasa. As always Beaver was very relaxed whenever she went in a vehicle.

I should have been excited with my new highly paid job with a large amount of responsibility. I was far from it. I tried to be kind and chatted to the driver about his family. In many ways the journey went too quickly I dreaded my arrival. It was after hours and so we went straight to Tim's house.

I got a friendly greeting from Hadi which lifted my spirits. Beaver flopped down on her blanket which I put on the veranda. Hadi told me that Tim was away on safari. I had a panic attack. Was I going to have to introduce myself on my own to the blond. With the help of the driver, we carried my stuff into one of the spare rooms. Hadi suggested that he made up the bed in the other spare room. Now I knew that Tim was definitely sleeping with the blond if they were sharing a bedroom. Presumably she had gone with him on safari. I tried ever so casually to ask Hadi if Tim's young lady had gone with him on safari. I was slightly relieved to hear that she had returned to England. The situation was going to be awkward but not quite as bad as I had been getting my knickers in a twist about. Suddenly all I could remember was that the last time I had been close to Tim I had not been wearing any knickers and he had just found out.

I resolved to stay calm. We had just had a wonderful evening out. We had been about to have a one-night stand and had been interrupted by an outbreak of rinderpest. End of story he had got together with his previous girlfriend, or he had hooked up with a new girl. Either way it was none of my business. I did not care anyhow, but I knew that I did care. In fact, if I was honest, I cared a great deal.

I was aware how much my Somali had improved as I chatted away to Hadi. I used very little English and no Swahili. He went into the kitchen to make supper and left me with my thoughts. I wondered if I had spoken on the radio to the Somalian Airforce jet, he would have broken off the action before causing me to crash. I gave an involuntary shiver just thinking about the incident and how lucky that I had been. I was surprised that I had had no consequent mental problems. I had not had one sleepless night. I thought I must be made of pretty stern stuff or that I was extremely stupid. I wondered why I was in such a turmoil about Tim. Perhaps I did love him. One thing for certain I definitely was not going to tell him. He had humiliated me by not being honest. Yet when I thought about it a little more. He had not really had the chance. I had rushed off into the eastern side of the NFD and he had gone to the western side. From then on, our paths had not crossed. All the veterinary radios were based in the eastern side of the NFD.

Anyway, that's how it had been. I wondered if it would have been any different if we had actually made love. Wow I had wanted to. I felt my whole-body blush. I realised that when he arrived home, if he made any advances regardless of the new girlfriend, I would give myself to him. What was wrong with me? I heard his Landrover arrive. I could not stop myself from getting up and walking to the door and out on to the veranda. Of course, Tim did not know that I was coming. He got out his Landrover and looked up and saw me at the same time as Beaver rushed out barking.

He had a broad grin on his face, "Well this is a lovely surprise."

To hide my feelings of desire, I snapped, "You abandoned me!" I did not want it to come out like that, but it did.

He looked perplexed. "Why are you so cross?"

I answered, "Now the blond has gone back to the UK, you are pleased to see me."

He infuriated me by still looking confused, "What you mean Angela."

I replied, "Yes, Angela, if that's what her name is."

I then burst into tears. He had every right to be cross with me. I was behaving like a spoilt teenager. However, he was kind he came towards me and took me in to his arms. To my shame when he kissed me, I returned his kiss. Then the words came tumbling out, "I saw you together at Mombasa airport. You looked so happy. She has such lovely legs. I was so upset I immediately enrolled to get my PPL."

He laughed then and asked. "Have you got it then."

I was still petulant, "Of course I have got it. I had to be able to fly something after the Somali jet wrote-off the microlight."

He looked concerned, "I can see you have a lot to tell me."

I replied, "Not until you tell me about Angela."

He answered, "There is not much to tell. You are right she has got good legs. She's my twin sister."

About the Author

I was born on a farm in 1944. I learnt to read at a local school but found it difficult. Mathematics on the other hand was very easy. I dreaded school work exercises like 'what was the most interesting thing that you did in the holidays'. I failed 'O' level English Language the first time around but passed English Literature.

I am a compulsive traveller. At five years of age I set my sights on Africa. Animals interested me, particularly farm and game animals. I spend a considerable amount of time with our elderly shepherd, Harry Weller, who was a very patient teacher. Other than my mother, he was the only person to cry, when having completed my veterinary degree at Bristol Veterinary School, I took up a post in Kenya. There was no TV. I read a large amount.

After eight years I returned to the UK and joined a practice in Norfolk where I have been ever since. I got married to Jane. Sadly our marriage only lasted twenty years but resulted in a son Henry an economist and a daughter Amelia a veterinary surgeon.

I have always been interested in disseminating knowledge and so I published in peer reviewed journals and wrote articles in veterinary newspapers. My doctorate asked the question, 'Does the veterinary profession need another peer reviewed journal?' History has agreed with my conclusion that it doesn't, only an improvement in the existing journals.

To find out more about Graham and his books:

Facebook - https://www.facebook.com/graham.duncanson.7

LinkedIn - http://linkedin.com/in/graham-duncanson-8624105b

All my novels are available from Amazon under
GRAHAM DUNCANSON.

Mating Lions by Graham Duncanson

In 1966 Jim Scott, aged 22, qualifies as a veterinary surgeon and lands the job of his dreams working in Kenya. Arriving in Kenya and knowing no one, he quickly makes friends.

His work involves travelling in the arid areas of Northern Kenya, carrying out a wide variety of veterinary jobs, as well as doing some clandestine spying for the British Government.

After a girl that he is fond of returns to England, he decides to learn to fly. This leads him into a seriously dangerous mission requested by his controller, the wife of the High Commissioner. When they eventually meet at a reception at the High Commission, it's a case of love at first sight. They go clandestinely together at day break to Nairobi Game Park and they are lucky to see two lions mating.

Their torrid affair ends in tragedy. Jim survives, but will he be mentally as well as physically scarred for life?

This is the first book of a trilogy.

Fiona by Graham Duncanson

In 1966 Jim Scott, aged 22, qualified as a veterinary surgeon and landed the job of his dreams working in Kenya. Just before leaving, he fell in love with Fiona, a Scottish girl, but there was no chance of a lasting relationship and they agreed to part.

Three and a half years later, Jim is mentally and physically scarred by a lion, which he kills with a *'panga'*, but not before it kills a woman he cares about.

At his wit's end working through the tragedy, Fiona comes out to Kenya. They find their love has not died, but Jim is too hung up on the past. Fi takes the lead and loves his fears away and they start planning a wedding and a family and their lives together.

Then, persuaded by a senior MI6 officer to gather information on their travels in Kenya and in other African countries, they face danger that could threaten everything they've worked for and dreamed of.

Fiona is book two of the Mating Lions Trilogy.

Francesca by Graham Duncanson

In 1939 in Northern Kenya, after an unpleasant incident with a German, a young Italian girl decides to throw in her lot with a young District Officer, Jack Harding.

She is actually half-English, and when her language skills are discovered by the Kenyan authorities, she and Jack, with the help of a group of Rendile tribesmen, thwart an attack by the Italians. During their adventures, the relationship between Francesca and Jack grows.

Jack enlists to fight the war and is rapidly promoted and posted to Burma, where he is captured by the Japanese and imprisoned in a POW camp.

Meanwhile, Francesca, who hates school in Nairobi and is expelled, turns his large house into a successful hotel.

She is summoned to London in 1946 by Sir Richard Harding as Jack, his youngest son, has now been declared, 'Missing believed dead'.

Francesca convinces Sir Richard that Jack may still be alive and she travels to Burma determined to try to find him.

Anna by Graham Duncanson

Anna is fourteen. She foolishly tries to rescues a zebra foal from a crocodile in Kenya. Her life is saved by a vet in his twenties who thinks she is in her gap year.

He takes her on a flight to watch him play rugby. She kisses him after the game, but she then has to return to the UK. Anna develops a passion for rugby and a determination to become a vet.

Four years later she comes to Kenya to find him. They travel in an old Landrover, overland through Europe and fall in love but there is a long road before them before they can hope to get married.

Katie by Graham Duncanson

It is 1964. Katie is eighteen and has trained to be an air hostess. She has just completed her first long haul flight to Kenya. Because of scheduling difficulties, the whole crew have been granted a seven night stopover and they decide to go on a minibus safari around the game parks.

Katie strongly resists the totally inappropriate advances of the senior captain and so he blocks her inclusion on the safari.

Left on her own, she meets Ian, a vet who is twelve years older than her. He appears to be kind and offers to take her on a really exciting safari to Northern Kenya. Their relationship develops and leads to some exciting escapades which would certainly have broken a weaker girl, both physically and mentally. Then Ian gets arrested on a trip to Iran. Katie requires all her fortitude to attempt a rescue.

Emily by Graham Duncanson

Emily is a farmer's daughter who had a passion to become a veterinary surgeon and go to work in Africa. She qualifies only to find that her small stature and her feminine good looks are against her. She is unable to secure employment.

She gets a break when her great aunt asks her to come out to Kenya and help her run her large ranch in the Northern Frontier District. Getting to the ranch is not easy. However her great aunt is very welcoming. Emily's world disintegrates around her when her great aunt dies during her first night on the ranch. She is befriended by Simon, a young, but more senior vet, who goes out of his way to help her. She falls in love with him, but he keeps her at arm's length.

Emily shows courage and fortitude. She gains respect not only from her employees on the ranch but also from the senior members of the Veterinary Department and the Government Administration.

She meets Simon's family and gains an insight into his character, but is this sufficient to earn his love?

Polly by Graham Duncanson

Polly is eighteen, when her father, a professional hunter, is killed by a wounded buffalo. Her mother died, when she was born. In theory she is totally on her own. However the Kenyans, who worked for her father and have known her all her life, are very loyal. She is determined to keep the business afloat to protect their jobs. Kenya has recently become independent and there is large scale unemployment.

When she finds out that her father had borrowed heavily from the bank and they are going to close the business down and make her bankrupt, she does not despair. She even considers selling herself to a wealthy rancher.

Will her beautiful smile and wonderful figure be enough for her to marry the older man she really loves?

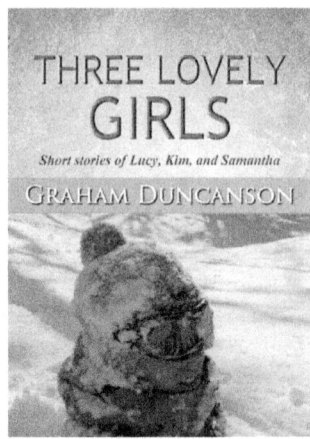

Three Lovely Girls by Graham Duncanson

Three short stories about three lovely girls in very different circumstances who fall in love.

It's Lucy's sixteenth birthday. She can never please her mother. She tries but somehow they are not on the same wavelength. A random meeting at the top of a ski run on Christmas Day leads her to a very exciting week, much to her mother's disapproval. Lucy despairs that her mother will never accept her new boyfriend.

Kim is totally fed up with her young stepmother. She decides to run away. Not a simple task as her father is the President of the USA. Help comes in the form of an old veterinary surgeon. Will they both escape and allow Kim to follow her dream.

Samantha is at her wits end. She is all alone in Norfolk just before Christmas. A chance meeting at the top of a church tower results in a job in a ski resort and an epic flight in a small plane to Kenya may cause more problems than it solves.

Lucy by Graham Duncanson

It's Lucy's sixteenth birthday. A random meeting at the top of a ski run on Christmas Day leads to a fast moving love affair. Her mother finds out that Lucy has spent the last night of the holiday with Peter. She calls Lucy a harlot and says she will never speak to her again. Her father normally takes Lucy's side but he fails to calm down his wife.

Lucy runs away from home to Scotland, mainly to save her parent's marriage. She learns to look after sheep, having rescued an elderly shepherd. She is very happy living with him and makes many, new friends. Her life takes a very rapid movement upwards after she rescues Lord Carmichael, Peter's grandfather from a car accident in a deep, cold, Scottish river. The question is, '*Will this lead her back to Peter*'?

The first chapter of *Lucy* was previously published as a short story in *Three Lovely Girls*.

Freda by Graham Duncanson

Set in the time of the 2017 Churchill film, *Darkest Hour*, we follow Gordon, a young British Officer in the King's African Rifles in 1939. He is sent off alone to try and gain intelligence for British Army on the possible Italian invasion of Kenya. He links up with Emma, Lord Wakefield's daughter who is half Italian. They experience some horrendous escapades with a camel called Freda, and fall in love. They get involved in the hostilities in the Western Desert. The chances of their survival appear to be remote. Can their love and courage save Cairo from the Axis Powers?

Jenny by Graham Duncason

Jenny is a newly qualified vet who having been a bit of a party girl at Cambridge has not achieved the academic results her professor would have wished. He is reluctant to pass her on her resit results. Jenny is offered a way into the profession by agreeing to go to work in Kenya, where they are desperate for field veterinarians. Jenny has always loved adventures and so going to Africa really appeals to her. She finds herself totally on her own in Mombasa on Christmas Eve.

Men, particularly older men, find her very attractive. On the whole they go out of their way to help her. However, she finds herself in a very challenging situation and has no one available to guide her. Her courage does not desert her and she copes admirably. She meets a pilot called Matt and they become very close friends, but sadly their relationship is going to be very short. Jenny is left alone and has to rely on her fortitude to get her out of a very dark place.

The Scream by Graham Duncanson

Jim Scott is a veterinary surgeon who worked in Kenya, having qualified in 1966. His early career is described in 'Mating Lions' and 'Fiona'. Fiona, the love of his life, dies of cancer in 2012.

He continues to practice in the UK, but his clandestine past catches up with him. He decides to set off on a bicycle ride from his home in Norfolk to Cape Town. He has many different companions riding with him in a relay to keep him company, including his five daughters.

After a logistical problem in Northern Kenya, he is on his own, when he faces the most dangerous part, not only of this journey, but also of his life.

This is the final book in the Mating Lions Trilogy.

Sarah by Graham Duncanson

As a very young girl, Sarah set her sights on Hector, who is ten years her senior. When he leaves Kenya aged eighteen to go to England to study to be a vet, she plucks up courage to kiss him.

By the time he returns she is much more mature and has her flying license. Their love quickly blossoms, but it is 1938 and war threatens everything. They know that they will have to part, but they take a giant leap of faith and get married.

Separately they face horrendous dangers. Their heroic efforts for the allied cause do not go unnoticed. Will Sarah's strength and fortitude save them both in the end?

Fighting for Liberty by Graham Duncanson

Libby is a newly qualified secret agent. On her first assignment she meets a retired agent who is three times her age, Jim Scott. There is an instant bond between them. They are thrown together trying to discover the traitor in their ranks. She learns a lot from him. It is only when she is alone without him that she realises how deeply she was in love with him. The story is an adventure of survival. Will she be able to put the past behind her and reach closure?

Ruth by Graham Duncanson

This is a rags to riches romance. Ruth, the heroine, was the daughter of a whore attached to The Duke of Wellington's Peninsular Army. She thinks that she was born in 1800. She hardly remembers her mother who died when she was only five years old. She follows the British army to Waterloo where she steals a horse and rescues a young, blinded, cavalry officer, who actually is Lord Chandos. They fall in love and with her help they arrive at his country seat, 'Stowe'. She bears him ten children who all play major roles in the story. Her mission is to help him to regain his sight.

Liberty Comes at a Price by Graham Duncanson

This is a stand alone novel but it does follow my previous novel 'Fighting for Liberty'.

Libby and her three colleagues, Kate, Rosemary and Gemma are given their most dangerous assignment to date. They carry out their task with ruthless efficiency. Other assignments follow until disaster strikes. Libby is left sad and alone. A man comes on to her radar, but they are not destined to make a life together. Will happiness always allude her?

The Sinners by Graham Duncanson

Two young Victorian teenagers in aristocratic Scotland fall in love, only to find out that they can never marry as they both have the same father. Far from feeling repugnance for each other, they can not stem their physical attraction. They strive to behave in society as brother and sister. In private they are sinners. They make an escape to East Africa where their liberal behaviour is tolerated rather than welcomed. They rescue some slaves and climb Mount Kilimanjaro. Only when they reach Voi in Kenya and The Great War is finished do they find real happiness.

Catherine's Crazy War by Graham Duncanson

One of Britain's spymasters, Bertie who is in his forties has been lusting after Catherine since he caught her swimming in the nude when she was sixteen.

Catherine is driven by the three Ps. She is patriotic, passionate and promiscuous. Bertie is happy to take her virginity on her request on her eighteenth birthday, the day when Britain declared war on Nazi Germany. She saves him from a certain assassination attempt. A bond is forged between them which all the dark aspects of war can not break.

The chances of either of them surviving the war are slight. The risks they are taking for their country are enormous and are requested at the highest level, not only in bomb torn London but also in many other theatres of the conflict.

Una Walks With The Elephants by Graham Duncanson

Una is a patriot. This is her diary. She uses her many talents to serve her country in The First World War. Her courage shines through in the mainly male dominated war.

First and foremost she was a nurse on the Western Front. Here she also learnt to tunnel with Welsh miners before becoming a sniper using her superb eyesight and terrifying accuracy with a rifle. Thus she was a natural with a Lewis gun in the primitive aircraft of the Royal Flying Corps. She becomes a pilot and destroys a Zeppelin over London Docks.

She meets her future husband, Ronald Nesbitt and they, as a duo, attempt to destroy the Turkish rail network in the Middle East. Tragically he dies in her arms.

She is lucky and is rescued by a Sheik before The British Military Intelligence require her services. The chances of her survival is remote after she sets off on a secret mission to East Africa.

Una's Second War by Graham Duncanson

Una's husband died in 'The Great War' in her arms. She meets James Robertson in the bush in Africa. She saves his life and without informing him selects him to be her second husband. She helps him to develop a very successful ranch in Kenya with the help of two African friends. She bears him three daughters.

James is captured at Dunkirk. Una needs the help of her youngest daughter. Their skills as aviators are required to effect his rescue. The whole family can then focus on, not only defeating the Nazis, but also exposing their heinous crimes against humanity.

Saving Lydia by Graham Duncanson

This is a love story between a young destitute publisher, Lydia and an old retired vet, Dick. It is set in the time of the Covid Pandemic. There is a very large age gap between them. Lydia is very depressed and Dick is lonely. However something sparks between them. They are in fact ideally suited as Dick is very sympathetic and understanding. He is a benevolent father figure which Lydia needs. They become very close as they are locked down together. Lydia actually is very adventurous and outward going. With his help she blossoms and her wicked sense of humour comes to the fore. They are reported to the police for committing incest and indecent behaviour. This is clearly seen as rubbish by the investigating police officers, who become their friends.

Dick teaches Lydia all about veterinary practice both in England and in Kenya. She appreciates his passion for flying and for rugby football. Dick's past catches up with him. Lydia does not hesitate to stand by him. They make a formidable pair.

Sylvie by Graham Duncanson

Sylvie is a French girl who has to endure the murder of her parents by the Gestapo on the day before D Day. She saves the lives of a British tank crew and manages to stay with them, when they are part of the force which liberates Paris. Disaster strikes when their squadron attempts to link up with the besieged parachute regiments who have been dropped on Arnhem. She nurses the tank squadron commander after she has rescued him, when he has been crushed by his tank. At the end of the war he is demobbed to England and he brings her with him. It is only then that she really becomes aware of his wealth and aristocratic origins.

Afsoon by Graham Duncanson

Afsoon escapes the Taliban in August 2021 having seen them murder her family. She escapes in the wheel arch of a transport plane and is found dying at Brize Norton. She survives and is befriended by an old dairy farmer who not only adopts her, but also teaches her to play cricket. She is passionate in her desire to be British. Her intelligence and her ability to play cricket enable her to get a place at Cambridge Veterinary School to read Veterinary Science. Her bravery and resilience insure her survival in a dangerous world. Will her courage and ability to reflect on her past lead her to a happy life?

Emma by Graham Duncanson

Emma was at home at the outbreak of the Second World War. She had received acceptance to go up to Oxford to read mathematics in a month's time. That was not to be. With the help of the security services, she was recruited by the RAF for a crucial role. The bait was that she was going to be trained to fight. That does not stop her falling in love.

Annabel's Vow by Graham Duncanson

A chance meeting by Annabel and Tom in a centre collecting first aid equipment for Ukraine in Norwich leads to a hair-raising trip in a transit van to Ukraine. This hardens Annabel's resolve to help the Ukrainian army to defeat the Russian invaders. The two become a formidable duo and have many successes.

Annabel is very circumspect in what she tells her parents. Her mother finds no problems with her spending her gap year in helping Ukrainian refugees. Little does her mother know that Annabel helps Tom and his associates to drop a bomb on the Russian command centre in Mariupol. Luck runs out for Tom who is killed. Annabel plans revenge.

Annabel Tries to Be Normal but Fails by Graham Dunanson

After a rather violent second half of her gap year, Annabel settles down at Oxford. However hard she tries she cannot seem to have a normal life. She is far from an average student as she learns to fly and falls in love with yet another man much older than herself. He like her is a skier. They have good times together on the slopes and on a holiday to Kenya. Then her world seems to crumble when he gets killed flying a light aircraft. Will she ever find lasting happiness?

Frostie Talks in the Shower by Graham Dunanson

Frostie and Richard meet in November 2022. They are both independent in their late twenties. They are brought together by a dog, Ruth, who is very special. She has been trained to guide blind people. Richard had been blinded while in the army on a special operation. Now he has left the army having been trained as a financial adviser.

There is an obvious attraction between them, but their professional careers raised many difficulties. Neither of them knew whether these problems were insurmountable. Would their time and adventures, together and apart, bring about more than just a friendship?

Printed in Great Britain
by Amazon